Dragon Night

Also from Donna Grant

Don't miss these other spellbinding novels!

Reaper Series

Dark Alpha's Claim
Dark Alpha's Embrace
Dark Alpha's Demand
Dark Alpha's Lover
Tall Dark Deadly Alpha Bundle
Dark Alpha's Night
Dark Alpha's Hunger

Dark King Series

Dark Heat (3 novella compilation)
Darkest Flame
Fire Rising
Burning Desire
Hot Blooded
Night's Blaze
Soul Scorched
Dragon King (novella)
Passion Ignites
Smoldering Hunger
Smoke And Fire
Dragon Fever(novella)
Firestorm
Blaze
Dragon Burn (novella)
Heat
Torched

Dark Warrior Series

Midnight's Master
Midnight's Lover
Midnight's Seduction
Midnight's Warrior
Midnight's Kiss
Midnight's Captive
Midnight's Temptation

Midnight's Promise
Midnight's Surrender (novella)

Dark Sword Series
Dangerous Highlander
Forbidden Highlander
Wicked Highlander
Untamed Highlander
Shadow Highlander
Darkest Highlander

Rogues of Scotland Series
The Craving
The Hunger
The Tempted
The Seduced

Chiasson Series
Wild Fever
Wild Dream
Wild Need
Wild Flame

LaRue Series
Moon Kissed
Moon Thrall
Moon Bound
Moon Struck

Shield Series
A Dark Guardian
A Kind of Magic
A Dark Seduction
A Forbidden Temptation
A Warrior's Heart

Druids Glen Series
Highland Mist
Highland Nights

Highland Dawn
Highland Fires
Highland Magic
Dragonfyre (connected)

Sisters of Magic Trilogy
Shadow Magic
Echoes of Magic
Dangerous Magic

Sons of Texas Series
The Hero
The Protector
The Legend

Heart of Texas Series
The Christmas Cowboy Hero
Cowboy, Cross My Heart

Dragon Night

A Dark Kings Novella

By Donna Grant

1001 Dark Nights

EVIL EYE
CONCEPTS

Dragon Night
A Dark Kings Novella
By Donna Grant

1001 Dark Nights
Copyright 2018 Donna Grant
ISBN: 978-1-948050-01-2

Foreword: Copyright 2014 M. J. Rose
Published by Evil Eye Concepts, Incorporated

Sign up for the 1001 Dark Nights Newsletter
and be entered to win a Tiffany Key necklace.

There's a contest every month!

Go to www.1001DarkNights.com to subscribe.

As a bonus, all subscribers will receive a free copy of
Discovery Bundle Three
Featuring stories by
Sidney Bristol, Darcy Burke, T. Gephart
Stacey Kennedy, Adriana Locke
JB Salsbury, and Erika Wilde

One Thousand and One Dark Nights

Once upon a time, in the future...

*I was a student fascinated with stories and learning.
I studied philosophy, poetry, history, the occult, and
the art and science of love and magic. I had a vast
library at my father's home and collected thousands
of volumes of fantastic tales.*

*I learned all about ancient races and bygone
times. About myths and legends and dreams of all
people through the millennium. And the more I read
the stronger my imagination grew until I discovered
that I was able to travel into the stories... to actually
become part of them.*

*I wish I could say that I listened to my teacher
and respected my gift, as I ought to have. If I had, I
would not be telling you this tale now.
But I was foolhardy and confused, showing off
with bravery.*

*One afternoon, curious about the myth of the
Arabian Nights, I traveled back to ancient Persia to
see for myself if it was true that every day Shahryar
(Persian: شهریار, "king") married a new virgin, and then
sent yesterday's wife to be beheaded. It was written
and I had read, that by the time he met Scheherazade,
the vizier's daughter, he'd killed one thousand
women.*

*Something went wrong with my efforts. I arrived
in the midst of the story and somehow exchanged
places with Scheherazade – a phenomena that had
never occurred before and that still to this day, I
cannot explain.*

Now I am trapped in that ancient past. I have taken on Scheherazade's life and the only way I can protect myself and stay alive is to do what she did to protect herself and stay alive.

Every night the King calls for me and listens as I spin tales. And when the evening ends and dawn breaks, I stop at a point that leaves him breathless and yearning for more. And so the King spares my life for one more day, so that he might hear the rest of my dark tale.

As soon as I finish a story... I begin a new one... like the one that you, dear reader, have before you now.

Prologue

Dreagan

February

How Dorian wanted to ignore the command, to pretend that he was too deep into the dragon sleep to hear the King of Dragon Kings.

But Con's voice penetrated even the deepest cloud of slumber.

"I promised I'd only wake you if there was no other way," Con said.

Dorian looked down at his hands—human hands. He'd never wanted to be in this form again. It was a reminder of all that he'd lost.

"We need you."

His head lifted to meet Con's black eyes. The last time they had stood thus, Dorian had been in a rage, inconsolable, and filled with vengeance. Several millennia had passed since, but to him, the pain was still unbearably raw.

Agonizingly visceral.

The King of Kings blew out a breath and absently turned a dragon head cufflink at his wrist. "I delayed until I couldna wait any longer, old friend."

"I know." Dorian's voice sounded odd to his ears. Rusty and rough from lack of use.

For the ones who slept, Con would visit each of the Kings every decade and use the special link between the dragons to fill each in on what was going on with the Kings, Fae, Druids, and mortals.

When the Dragon Kings' enemies began closing in, Con came to see Dorian every day to keep him up to date. Dorian had known then it would only be a matter of time before Con demanded that he wake and join them.

But Dorian still wished there was another way.

Yet, these dragons were his brethren. They had all suffered in one way or another, each believing their pain superceded all others.

Out of all the Kings, there were only two who didna wake every few centuries—V and Dorian. It was better this way. Everyone knew it.

V because he couldn't cope with the theft of his sword—a sword that was detrimental to the Dragon Kings.

And Dorian because he could never forgive the humans. Seeing one would likely result in their death.

Con's gaze lowered to the floor of the cavern before sliding to the large pool of water. He took a deep breath and met Dorian's eyes. "Take a day or two. Talk to the other Kings, walk the grounds, and learn the technology that governs the mortals."

"You didna tell me to meet the mates." Dorian was pushing Con, but he couldn't help himself. He was angry, and he needed to lash out at someone.

Better Con than a human.

"Nay, I didna. There are some at the manor who have yet to undergo the ceremony."

"Like Ulrik's mate, Eilish." Dorian watched Con closely to see if there was even a hint of worry in his old friend's eyes.

Con gave a single nod. "Aye."

"You think I would harm them?"

"They are humans."

Dorian dragged in a deep breath before slowly releasing it. "But they're the mates of my brethren."

"Can you distinguish between the two? We both know how deep your hatred runs."

"And yet you wish to send me out into a world filled with them."

When Con didn't immediately reply, Dorian took a step toward him, his stomach churning with apprehension.

Con slipped his hands into the pockets of his trousers. "It's worse than that."

"What are you no' telling me?"

"The object we want you to retrieve is in a private collection. I've tried to buy it, but I've been refused."

Dorian shrugged. "So? Any King can use their magic to retrieve it. You doona need me."

"If it were that easy, old friend, I would've gone myself."

Dorian crossed his arms over his chest. "I want to know all of it."

"Fine. You know about these new enemies of Fae and Druids aligning against us. Ryder scoured the web and found an artifact that dates back to our war with the humans."

"I'm sure that isna the only thing he found."

Con lifted one shoulder in a shrug. "It's the only one we know of. From the black and white pictures Ryder obtained, there are Fae markings on it."

Now that got Dorian's attention. "If they are Fae markings, then it would prove that they were here long before they claim to have arrived."

"Exactly. It'll also be the evidence we need to link the Fae to the Druids with the wooden dragon. I believe Rhi, but none of us can get near enough to the carving to determine what magic is being used. Without her, we wouldna even know this much."

Dorian still wasn't convinced he was the one for the job. "I suppose this is when you tell me why I'm the one to retrieve this artifact?"

"It's no' only under the tightest security the mortals have, but it's also surrounded by magic."

"And how do you know this?"

Con's lips flattened as he sighed. "Because Eilish tried to get it for us. Her finger rings allow her to teleport, and while she managed to get in the room, the magic threw her out. Then Ulrik tried. He got closer, but still wasna able to get to the object."

"Can we no' ask one of the Fae?" Dorian purposefully didn't say Rhi's name. He knew many of the Kings thought of her as a friend, but he didn't know the Light.

Con hesitated before he shook his head. "This group of Druids and Fae has targeted us, and me specifically. I want to know why before something else happens. And understand, Dorian, that something else is surely to occur. It's not a matter of if, but a matter of *when*. You're the only one who will be able to get through all the security and magic to reach the artifact. Your magic of invisibility allows you to bend matter to go undetected so you can go through anything."

"Getting it, however, will be another issue. You know I'll no' be able touch it while concealed."

Con didn't appear fazed by the statement. "I'm sending you to get this artifact, Dorian. We're no' thieves. Unless we have no other choice. I'd like to see if you can buy it from the mortal first. If that doesna work, then get it any way you can."

Dorian watched as Con turned on his heel and walked from the cavern. He might not have been involved in the many battles or daily machinations of the ongoing conflicts with their enemies, but that didn't mean Dorian hadn't felt the anger and desolation when his brethren had lost or the contentment and delight when they won.

In every word Con uttered while detailing everything, Dorian perceived his worry, his unease. But more than that, Dorian *felt* the fear that ran through Dreagan at their new nemesis.

Whoever this band of Dark and Light Fae and *drough* and *mie* Druid, their first strike had been substantial. The ramifications of the Kings touching the wooden dragon still caused ripples, and likely would for some time.

Dorian rolled his shoulders. His muscles were stiff from his time sleeping. Whether in dragon or human form, he needed to remember who he was.

He'd be happy to remain in his true form forever, but his King called for him. And that meant Dorian was going to have to interact with the very beings he wanted to wipe from the realm.

Slowly, he walked to the water. His enhanced eyesight didn't need the aid of any light as he peered over the edge to look at himself.

As soon as he saw his face, he cringed and jerked back. He wasn't prepared for this. But there wasn't time for him to get ready.

Dorian blew out a breath. The last time he had been outside his mountain was after he watched his dragons cross the dragon bridge to a new realm and helped to bind Ulrik's magic.

He'd been inconsolable, his world shattered in the space of a heartbeat. Everything he'd loved, everything he'd lived for had been taken from him. Viciously. Cruelly.

Ruthlessly.

Con had brought him to his mountain because Con knew if Dorian was left alone that he would finish what Ulrik had begun.

There wasn't a day that went by that Dorian didn't dream of his life before the humans.

Or plot their demise.

Now Con wanted him out in the world. Dorian would get what was needed to battle their new foes, but every chance he got, he would take out a mortal.

They didn't belong on this realm. It wasn't theirs. It belonged to the dragons.

And the dragons would take it back.

Soon. Very soon.

Dorian shifted and spread his wings as he shook his head. Then he drew in a deep breath before blowing fire across the water.

He jumped into the air and flew through the opening at the side of the mountain and felt the sunlight on him for the first time in eons. It warmed his scales while causing him to blink against its brightness.

Dorian flew as high as he could until the clouds blocked any sight of land. Then he glided down, the feel of the wind across his scales as heavenly as a lover's caress.

He soared between mountains, over lochs, and chased a herd of sheep. Then he saw the Dragonwood. He flew over the expanse of forest several times. Then he turned and headed for Dreagan Mountain.

The manor that came in sight was as grand as it was beautiful—but Con wouldn't build anything less.

A flash of jade scales caught his eye. He looked over to find Warrick flying next to him. When Dorian glanced to his other side, it was to see Kiril.

"Nice to have you back with us," Warrick said through the mental link of the dragons.

Kiril bumped him with his wing. *"I second that. It's been too long, brother."*

Dorian didn't know how to reply. He was still getting used to the sun and sky again. It seemed everyone else had moved on—including Ulrik. Was he the only one continuing to hold on to the past?

Was he the only one still hurting from what the humans had done?

"Dorian?" Warrick called.

"The sun feels good," he replied.

Kiril chuckled. *"There's the Dorian we know and love. You just missed V. He and Roman left to find his sword."*

Dorian remained silent as his two friends spoke about technology he didn't understand, vehicles, and flying machines. He frowned at that. Why did the Kings need a...helicopter? They could fly.

The fact that Dreagan had two such machines was a reminder of the lengths the great Dragon Kings had gone to in order to hide from the humans.

Both his friends were mated now. Kiril to a Fae and Warrick to a Druid. Fae and Druid. Surely he wasn't the only one to see the connection.

A King had a Fae as a mate. A Light Fae who had once been Dark. Then there were the Druids. Warrick's mate wasn't the only one. Ryder, Dmitri, Anson, Nikolai, and even Ulrik were with women who were either Druids or had some kind of connection to them.

Then there was Rhi.

The Light Fae who had fallen for a Dragon King and once their affair finished, remained friends with several Kings.

Con had always feared another betrayal. There was a massive one in the making, and no one but Dorian seemed to realize it.

He had a chance to stop it, to right things as they should've been to begin with.

And he was going to take it.

Chapter One

Manhattan, New York

March

"Oh, my God. Look at that dress."

"Girl. I'm looking at the jewels."

"Ugh. If only we had the Sheridan money we could buy whatever we wanted."

"I hear the stores come to her. She doesn't even shop on her own."

Alexandra rolled her eyes. It went against everything she'd been taught not to show in New York society, but sometimes the only thing to do when hearing others talk about you was to give an eye roll—even if it was just to herself.

Those two women were right. Wealth did have its privileges. Every American designer wanted Alex to wear their things, she was able to give a shitload of money to charities, and she was invited to all the parties.

The downside of being wealthy was that she was invited to all the parties. Not to mention the list of charity galas and other such events she was expected to attend.

Alex had never known anything other than the Sheridan fortune, which was probably why her mother used to give one of her famous eye rolls every time Alex would say she wished for a quiet life in the country somewhere.

"If only," Alex murmured.

But her destiny lay elsewhere. She was the sole remaining member of the Sheridan dynasty. She lived alone in a huge penthouse while overseeing the ridiculous fortune made by her great-great-great grandfather when he came over from Ireland.

She moved to the back of the stage and grabbed a flute of champagne from a passing waiter. After last year's disaster, she'd sworn never to do the auction again. But what was she about to do?

Put herself back up on that stage while smiling and flirting to get the bids higher. All in the name of charity.

Her cousin had died in some remote part of the world she couldn't pronounce defending their country. So, no matter how degrading it felt, or how horrible the "date" was, she would never turn down the Wounded Warrior charity for veterans. Especially since she sat on the Board of Directors.

"It's time, Alex."

She turned at the sound of her assistant's voice. Meg had been with her for three glorious years. It was Meg who kept her sane—as well as keeping her on a schedule that didn't run Alex into the ground.

She smiled into Meg's black eyes as she leaned close and grinned. "I didn't get a chance to tell you when you walked away earlier, but the bartender totally checked out your ass. I told you that you seriously rock it in that fuchsia dress with your dark skin. You look like a goddess."

Meg shifted and covertly glanced toward the bartender, who was even now eying her. "Then I suppose I should tell you that he asked me out when I was getting you a drink."

"I've got one," Alex said.

Meg gave her a flat look. "Of course. But I was giving studly a chance to ask me out."

"Of course you were."

They shared a laugh.

Alex knew it was dangerous to become friends with someone she employed, but the truth was, Meg was her only friend. Alex had learned at a very young age that people only wanted to be her friend in order to get something from her. Whether it be station, items, or money—everyone had a reason for wanting to be with her.

Consequently, she had trust issues. It also didn't help that the few times she had attempted to trust someone, it had ended with them using her in one fashion or another. Frankly, she was tired of it.

While others coveted her wealth, Alex was jealous of their relationships, of the way they could walk along the street without paparazzi following their every move.

Which left her Meg. They had hit it off instantly. But even then, Alex tried to stay as detached as she could. Just in case.

She followed Meg to the stairs that led to the stage. No matter how many speeches she gave, she always got nervous anytime she had to stand in front of a group of people.

Because everyone was picking her apart. From her hair, makeup, jewelry, and nails to the way she stood, if it looked as if she'd gained weight, and every word she said.

Was it any wonder that between her social engagements she disappeared for weeks at a time to try and forget the spotlight that was always on her?

"Welcome, ladies and gentlemen!"

Alex looked up as the emcee for the event came on stage. She didn't know the news anchor, Lori Duval, personally, but she'd suggested a female host this year, and it had been approved by the rest of the Board. By the sound of the applause, everyone else seemed pleased by the change as well.

"I'm very excited to be here," Lori said as the overhead lights made the rhinestones in her dress glitter. "My grandfather, father, two brothers, and five cousins have or are serving this fine country of ours. I've long been a donor to this amazing charity. You all know the drill," she replied with a bright smile. "Every penny earned here goes straight into the Wounded Warrior project. If there was one night for you to open those pocketbooks, it's tonight. Now, why don't we get this party started?"

The crowd laughed, but all Alex wanted to do was turn and run. Her stomach clutched painfully and her blood had turned to ice.

Meg physically removed the champagne flute from her fingers before Alex snapped it in two. Sadly, it had happened before.

"Breathe," Meg urged.

Alex inhaled deeply, but before she could let it out, Lori said her name.

With no other choice, Alex placed her hand on the railing and walked up the steps on wooden legs. Her greatest fear was that she would trip and fall during one of these events.

People might talk, but she was used to that. She didn't want them laughing at her - at least not for something as stupid as falling.

Before she knew it, she was standing next to Lori. The news anchor was talking, but Alex didn't hear any of it. She faced the crowd and smiled. There were several whistles, which caused laughter to erupt around the room.

"Wow," Lori said as she looked at Alex. "I guess we should've known that would happen. Everyone wants to date Alexandra Sheridan. Even me."

Alex smiled and winked at Lori. Years of being in the spotlight kicked in, and she leaned into the microphone. "I go to the top bidder. If you want a chance, you know what you need to do."

Lori acted like she was looking around for her purse. Then she said to the crowd, "You heard her, ladies and gents. Who is going to start this auction off for a date with New York's most eligible bachelorette, Alexandra Sheridan?"

"Five thousand," a man shouted from the back.

Alex kept a smile on her face, clapping with the others each time the amount rose. She wondered what animals at auction thought as they stood there while others bid on them. She had to keep telling herself it was for a good cause.

The bidding went on longer than it had the year before. It was up to forty thousand when a deep voice from somewhere in the middle of the room said, "A hundred thousand."

A shiver raced through Alex at the seductive tone.

The silence that followed was deafening.

The spotlight slid across the room and came to rest on a man leaning against the bar. Their eyes met, and her heart literally skipped a beat.

He was in a tux, but only the top portion. And as she took in the kilt, she had to admit, he looked as sexy as sin.

The light above him shone on his blond hair, pulled back into a neat queue at the base of his neck. He had some ornate thing draped around his hips, but all she could think about was if he had anything on beneath the kilt.

"Sold!" Lori suddenly shouted, causing Alex to jump.

The man turned and set his glass on the bar. Alex blinked before she made her way back to the stairs and Meg.

"Might I just say holy shit," Meg whispered with a grin.

Alex stopped, only dimly aware that the next person was up on the stage being auctioned. "What just happened?"

"Somebody bid an extreme amount for you."

Meg was smiling, her gaze telling Alex that she wasn't sure why Alex wasn't thrilled. But then again, Meg hadn't seen the man.

"What's wrong?" her assistant asked.

"He's...different."

Meg raised a black brow. "Do you know him?"

"No."

"Have you met him?"

"Well, no," Alex began.

But Meg continued. "Then you can't really say that he's different."

Alex recalled the man's stare. It had been bold, defiant even. And determined. Yes, determined was a very good word to describe him. He'd stood alone, as if he didn't know anyone—or care that he was by himself.

His entire appearance gave off the vibe of "fuck you, I'm going to get what I want."

A shiver went through Alex once again. Men like that were particularly difficult to handle. They never really understood the word no.

"I've never seen him before," Alex said.

Meg's gaze was directed toward the crowd. "I think everyone is figuring that out. Oh, my," she whispered. "Is that a *kilt*?"

"Yes."

"I thought I heard an accent. Hard to tell with only three words." Meg swallowed loudly. "You know I have a thing for Outlander. If you don't want him, can I have him?"

"Um..."

"He's paying for you," Meg went on, her entire focus on the stranger.

Alex grabbed another glass of champagne from a tray and took a long drink. The bubbles did little to squash the nerves in her stomach.

The past four years she had done this auction, she'd always ended up with men that she knew. Men that had asked her out on a date and she had turned down. This was their revenge in making her go out with them.

Which was fine with her as long as the charity got its money.

"He's got that Jamie Fraser look down pat," Meg murmured.

Alex rolled her eyes and snagged a napkin. "Here."

Meg reluctantly pulled her gaze from the man and frowned. "What's that for?"

"The drool."

Meg huffed and snatched the napkin from Alex's fingers. Her lips curved into a grin as her gaze returned to the man.

"He's the sexiest thing I've ever seen."

Alex shook her head. "You say that once a week."

"This time I mean it." Meg suddenly whirled around to Alex. "He caught me staring. Oh, and by the way, he's coming over here."

Unable to help herself, Alex lifted her eyes and found herself snagged by his gaze.

Chapter Two

She was magnificent. Dorian hadn't expected that. Her beauty, of course. He'd seen a picture before he left Scotland—as well as getting a complete background review from Ryder.

But Alexandra Sheridan was anything but a typical woman.

The way she had stood on the stage looking out over the crowd with grace and calm shocked him. She was of average height, but that was the only average thing about her.

Striking hazel eyes took in all with a glance. Everyone attempted to gain her attention just to have her look their way.

Her oval face and full, pouty lips had men and women alike panting after her. She wore some expensive dress. While Dorian didn't care about the brand, he quite liked how the fabric molded to her hourglass figure.

He didn't want to like her. In fact, he'd taken an instant aversion once he learned of her fortune. Dorian knew full well how mortals liked to acquire social standing through their wealth.

Except...he'd formed an opinion of Alexandra before he'd even seen her in person. Walking around the charity event, all he'd heard was praise about her. If anyone spoke negatively, it was because they coveted her wealth—or her—and nothing more.

To find a human who wasn't corrupt or deceitful in some way was an oddity. Everyone had some failing. And he intended to find out what Ms. Sheridan's was so he could use it against her to acquire the artifact.

He finished with the event host, and with a nod, turned to locate his purchased date. When Con originally told Dorian he was going to have to bid on Alexandra to get a date with her, he thought it ridiculous.

Then he learned from Ryder that Alexandra Sheridan didn't date. Anyone.

Her last boyfriend had been over four years ago, and it had ended in a scandal when he tried to sell her grandmother's heirloom gold candlesticks. Apparently, Alexandra knew he'd stolen them, but she hadn't called the police. It wasn't until after he was discovered that she pressed charges.

Why hadn't she immediately called the authorities? Why had she let him get away with it?

Dorian discovered the answer to that just by observing her. She was courteous and polite, but she kept herself detached from others.

Her assistant, a beautiful black woman with large, expressive eyes that could cut a person in their tracks, was always near Alexandra, putting herself between the world and her boss.

There was also a four-man security detail. They didn't bother trying to blend in. They stood out in their black suits with their white shirts and black ties and earpieces, looking imposing and threatening.

Dorian wanted to laugh. There wasn't anyone in the room—hell, in the world—that could stop him from getting to Alexandra Sheridan.

His gaze scanned the large room of men in tuxes and women dressed in evening wear draped in jewels until he caught sight of Alexandra's blond locks.

He had to admit that he quite liked her hair. She didn't hide her curls. In fact, she embraced them. Whether on purpose or accident, the coils fell around her face and neck from the soft updo.

She wore impressive diamond earrings that dropped down to brush against her bare shoulders. There was a diamond bracelet on her left wrist while a large diamond ring adorned her right hand.

Her gaze suddenly lifted and met his. Just as when she had looked his way after he'd won the bid, there was a beat of unease before she quickly masked it.

Alexandra Sheridan didn't know it yet, but her world was about to get turned upside down.

Dorian made his way toward her. He didn't have to move around others. They parted to let him through. He never took his eyes off his mark. He wanted her to know that she was his—so that she would realize trying to run was futile.

In less than a week since being woken, he was standing in a room of his enemies and he hadn't killed anyone. Yet. Con would be proud.

Hell, he was proud of himself.

It was easy since no one got near him, but that would change when he met Alexandra for their "date." It had been literally eons since he'd wooed anyone. Now he had to do it with one of the beings that he despised with every fiber of his soul.

But it was for Con and the rest of his brethren.

He couldn't—and wouldn't—say no to that.

As he neared Alexandra, she squared her shoulders and stood straight, her clutch held in one hand while her other grasped a champagne flute. It wasn't one of her genuine smiles that she bestowed upon him. But rather one that was polite, fake.

And that angered him.

"Hello," she said when he stopped before her. "I believe you shocked everyone with your bid. Thank you for your generosity. The funds will go a long way to helping veterans in need."

A dozen replies filled his head and fell upon his tongue, but he said none of them. For they would get him nowhere with the heiress.

Instead, he crafted another reply. One that would charm her, just as Con had urged him to do.

Dorian took a deep breath, and inwardly winced when he heard the words that fell from his lips. "Do I scare you, Ms. Sheridan?"

She blinked, utterly taken aback. "I...of course not."

"Your eyes say otherwise." He might not have meant to ask her such a question, but her response certainly intrigued him.

She glanced at her assistant, who had moved a few steps away. Alexandra then sighed. "I don't run across men like you."

"Men like me?" he repeated. "In a kilt?"

"With such blatant intention in their gaze," she said in a whisper, glancing around to see if others heard her.

Honesty. How about that? It was Dorian's turn to be taken aback. "Based on the way the bidding was going for you, there were quite a few men who let their intentions be known."

"I've not seen you around before."

"I'm new to the area."

She nodded. "What do you think of us?"

"You really want to know?"

"I do," she replied after a brief hesitation.

Dorian shifted to look back at the humans, all of whom were either outright staring, or trying to covertly look their way. "I think this is a room full of people with too much bloody money, but at least they're giving some of it to a worthwhile cause."

"What of your money?"

His head swung back to meet her hazel gaze. He grinned then. "I'm happy to give it away."

She held out her hand. "Alexandra Sheridan. Nice to meet you."

"Dorian," he replied as he took her hand in his.

He didn't shake it or kiss it. He simply held it while staring into her eyes.

"Dorian," she repeated. "No surname?"

He smiled and released her. "I believe I won a date with you, Ms. Sheridan. When would you like to go?"

Alexandra looked to her assistant, who quickly closed the distance separating them and handed Alexandra an iPad with a schedule pulled up.

"I've got an opening in two weeks," she told him.

That would never do. Not only did Dorian have serious reservations about remaining that long among mortals, but he wanted this mission completed as quickly as possible.

"Tomorrow," he said.

Her assistant snorted, a smug look on her face as she looked at Dorian. He ignored her as his gaze slid to Alexandra, who was frowning at him.

"Tomorrow? Um...that's not a good day for me."

"Perhaps that's your problem, lass," he said. "You need to do something for you instead of for others."

She blinked twice, her frown deepening. "I can't just cancel plans."

"People do it all the time," he retorted.

Her assistant lowered the iPad, confident that Alexandra would remain unmovable.

Dorian, however, wasn't going to go down that easily. "When was the last time you had a day just for you?" he asked.

Alexandra briefly looked away. "It's been awhile. Then again, I won't really have a day just for me. I'll be with you."

"Only for a few hours."

There was a lengthy pause as Alexandra stared at him. Then she said, "Meg, move my schedule around tomorrow."

"Alex?" Meg questioned, her face lined with confusion. "Are you sure?"

She looked to Meg and nodded. "I owe Dorian his date, and since he isn't from around here, I don't want to keep him waiting. It's just courtesy to give him what he demands."

"Thank you," Dorian said with a bow of his head.

He then opened the mental link and called Ryder's name. The Dragon King, who was also a tech guru in the truest sense of the word, answered immediately.

"Everything all right?"

Dorian smiled at Alex. *"Aye. I have a date with Alexandra Sheridan tomorrow. Let Con know that I'll be ready to return home in the next few days."*

"Are you sure you want to rush this?" Ryder asked. *"It has been awhile since you've used your charm."*

"I can handle it. There's no need to prolong this. I'm with her now. I'll do a walkthrough of her house tonight as I'd planned. If the opportunity is there, I'll take the object."

"I wanted you to offer for it first. Besides, she'll know it's you."

"So?"

"So that means she'll track you to Dreagan, dumbass. We doona need that scrutiny now."

Dorian sighed. *"Fine. But I think it's silly to even have me meet her."*

"We explained this before you left."

"Aye, I know. We're no' thieves," Dorian replied, cutting him off. *"If you had gone with my plan, no one would've seen me or been able to trace anything back to Dreagan. Just relay my message to Con."*

Dorian cut off the link. He didn't think the plan Con and Ryder had come up with was doable, but that was probably because he didn't like mortals.

But the Dragon Kings had worked long and hard to craft their current image. The least he could do was keep in line with that. So he'd give Con's plan a go. If that didn't work, he would fall back to Plan B.

Dorian smiled when he spotted Meg giving him a dark look. The assistant didn't like that he'd so easily manipulated Alex to change her schedule. That was too bad, but Meg needed to get used to it.

"Why me?"

Dorian had forgotten that he was standing with Alex. There had been a comfortable silence—at least on his part. "Excuse me?"

"Why did you buy me? There are dozens of other women up for bid tonight. And you probably should have gotten one of them, because if you think I'm going to give you an-"

"I doona assume anything, Ms. Sheridan," he said. "If I'd wanted a woman to warm my bed, I wouldna have to buy them."

She licked her lips.

"As for why I chose you," he continued. "It's because I want to know the woman who spends her life in New York society, but who doesna let anyone close."

"I fear you'll be disappointed then," she stated coolly.

He grinned. "Oh, I doubt that. Besides, I've learned quite a lot about you already."

Chapter Three

He stood atop the skyscraper, lifted his face to the wind, and closed his eyes. Dorian loved the sun, but there was something magical about nighttime.

The moon, the stars...the darkness.

With a sigh, he opened his eyes and grimaced at the sounds of sirens, honking horns, and just general noise that reached him.

New York City was too loud and too harsh for him. He wanted to cover his ears. Or fly up so high that he couldn't hear the dreadful racket.

He longed for the quiet of Dreagan. Where the only sounds were those of his brethren. If only it was the beat of wings or the roars of other dragons. Now those sounds he loved with all his heart.

Dorian used his magic and made himself invisible before shifting. The long talons of his feet sank into the stone, causing bits to crumble. He let himself fall to the side and immediately spread his wings.

Many of the buildings were too close so he had to fly sideways, but he still wound his way through the city. He gazed down at the people knowing how easy it would be to let loose dragon fire and wipe them away.

Nothing was hotter than dragon fire. The mortals would die before they even knew what hit them.

It was so tempting. So very, very tempting.

It was humans who had destroyed the dragons' way of life. It was the magic-less, weak mortals who had taken away everything he'd known and loved.

Dorian knew Con wanted to remain hidden and not bring about

another war with the humans. But no matter how many times Dorian told himself to let go of his anger, he couldn't.

His dragons had been more than his clan. Each and every one of them had been family—whether they were blood or not. He relived the day he'd ordered them to follow the others off the realm over and over again. And each time was like pouring salt into a wound.

More so knowing that the land that had been his to rule, the land that his dragons had called home, was now occupied by humans.

This realm was the dragons'.

Not the mortals'.

The more he flew around the city, the more he saw the destructive, weak actions of the mortals, the more he knew the realm would be better off without them.

He drew in a deep breath, ready to release his dragon fire when he spotted blond curls. Dorian knew immediately that it was Alexandra Sheridan without seeing either Meg who walked beside her, or the four bodyguards who surrounded her.

All thoughts of death evaporated. Dorian swung around to follow Alex after she got into the car and drove away. He knew where she lived, but he kept pace with her.

When they reached the Sheridan building, he perched on the top and watched as her door was opened by one of the guards before one long, slim leg emerged from the vehicle.

Once she was out, another bodyguard came to stand on the other side of the door, flanking her. Alex took a step and then Meg climbed out. In a blink, the other two guards brought up the rear.

Dorian snorted at the thought of such a show just ten steps outside of the building. But no sooner had that thought gone through his head than someone rushed toward Alex.

Two of the guards stopped the male assailant while the other two got Alex inside. Dorian frowned when he saw the light glint off a long blade in the attacker's hand before he was forced to drop it.

Dorian watched as a police car drove up with lights flashing, tires skidding as the vehicle quickly stopped. The man was placed in handcuffs and ceremoniously hauled off in the cruiser.

Only then did Dorian's mind turn back to Alex. He'd intended to come when everyone had gone to bed, but he found himself curious about how Alex was handling the attack.

Dorian returned to his human form, though he remained invisible.

He scaled down the side of the building until he reached the balcony. Alex's home took up the entire top floor, with the balcony encompassing the entire building.

It wasn't a skinny terrace either. It was spacious. Some parts had lounge areas with chairs and fire pits. Other portions were dedicated to various plants and potted trees.

He made his way around the balcony looking in windows. From what little he'd witnessed from the wealthy, he expected the decorations to be garish and tacky. Yet he discovered that Alexandra preferred a homier style.

The couch had creases in brown leather from years of use. There was a large TV hanging on the wall and a white furry rug that filled the space between the TV and the couch.

On the end tables and coffee tables were succulents—some of the plants big and some of the smaller ones clustered together. On either side of the television were shelves filled with so many movies that he wondered if she had actually watched them all.

A beige and white pillow sat against one corner of the couch along with a fur throw in shades of beige, white, and brown.

The room looked to be well used, and obviously one that Alex enjoyed. When Dorian moved around to the dining area, he could tell this wasn't a room that saw a lot of use.

The glass-topped table had eight chairs covered in white fabric. The base of the table looked like two column toppers.

Behind the dining area was the kitchen. It was immaculate, like everything else. Black stainless steel appliances, a double refrigerator, white quartz countertops with pale cabinets. The bar had three stools tucked neatly away.

Dorian continued on until he found three empty bedrooms and then an office—once more with nothing out of place. Not even a piece of paper on the desk.

Next, he found Alex in her bedroom. She sat on a large, round stool in her closet while taking off her shoes. Meg was pacing back and forth, obviously upset over the attack.

But Alex didn't seem fazed by any of it. She put away her shoes and stood. Then she told Meg she was done for the day. His advanced hearing picked up the soft words through the windows. His gaze shifted to the assistant, who gave a nod and walked to the door. Meg paused and looked over her shoulder. Alex gave her a smile and a wave of reassurance.

It wasn't until Meg was out of the flat that Alex walked to the large windows and moved aside the sheer curtains. Then she opened the sliding door and stepped out onto the balcony.

Dorian moved out of the way as she walked to the railing. She wrapped her arms around herself and stared out over the city, but he didn't think she was seeing the lights or the skyline.

It began with a tremor that he thought was a chill caused by the night air. Then the first tear fell. It wasn't long before her shoulders shook from the force of her crying. Alex dropped her chin to her chest and covered her face with her hands as she wept.

He stood with her, unsure of why he didn't move away. There was something about her silent suffering that touched him. For once, his constant anger paused, allowing his grief and misery to surface.

For those few minutes, two people stood in the moonlight, sunk in misery and heartache—and utterly alone in a city of millions.

Suddenly, she sniffed and lifted her head as she let her arms fall to her sides. Her gaze stared out over the skyscrapers while the tears on her face dried. Then she squared her shoulders and took a deep breath, as if finding her footing in the storm of emotions.

She turned and made her way back inside. He watched her head toward the bathroom wondering if she left the door open on purpose or not.

He slipped inside and made his way to the portion of the house he hadn't seen yet. His feet paused when he spotted her taking off her makeup. It was an ordinary chore, but one he hadn't witnessed before. He took in the array of many bottles on the counter, watching as she picked up one after the other to use.

He shook himself, remembering why he was there. He walked past the bathroom. The cameras—both seen and unseen—were everywhere. He was glad Ryder had taught him what to look for. Otherwise, there would be many places he wouldn't know a camera sat. But with his invisibility, he was able to move about undetected.

Ryder had cautioned him that some equipment was based on body temperature, so Dorian couldn't just stroll through the artifacts.

When he turned the corner and saw the room, he halted. It was like walking into a museum. Some pieces were encased in Plexiglas on a column with the name of the artifact and all information below it. Others hung on the wall or were in a large case with other artifacts.

Dorian walked through the first lasers and waited for the alarms to sound. When nothing happened, he made his way through the maze of objects until he found the piece he'd come for. The pictures Ryder and Con had showed him didn't do it justice.

It was an oblong object of about six inches in length. Dorian didn't care what was on the artifact. He simply wanted to get it and bring it back to Scotland so Con and the others could figure out what to do.

Dorian knew he wasn't leaving the city without it. Con wanted him to do things one way. Well, Dorian would try his king's plan. But if it didn't work, he was going to do this his way.

He retraced his steps, uncaring about the other items. Just as he was heading out of Alex's room, he heard water. His head turned toward the bathroom and he caught a glimpse in the mirror of a long arm with suds sliding down it.

His feet turned, and before he realized it, he stood in the bathroom looking at Alex with her curls piled on her head and her body covered with bubbles. Her head was back against the tub with her eyes shut. Music played from somewhere.

In one short night, he'd seen many sides of Alexandra Sheridan. And if he had to guess, the one he witnessed at that moment wasn't one that she showed anyone. The lonely, despondent side was kept carefully tucked away from others.

Much like his emotions.

In some ways, she was as trapped as the Dragon Kings. He didn't like making that connection, but there was no denying it. Her wealth and standing forced her into circumstances beyond her control. Just as the Kings still experienced.

Her eyes suddenly opened and looked right at him. He saw the flecks of gold in her hazel orbs, a curious and beguiling mix of green, gold, and brown.

He couldn't help but wonder what she would do if she knew he was there. What would she say? The openness, the vulnerability she wore now would vanish. Her mask of indifference, kindness, or strength would return.

Dorian knew all about masks. He'd been wearing once since he walked from his mountain a week ago. Inside, he raged, he seethed. And he plotted.

Behind Alex's mask, he saw something different. Loneliness, fear, and acceptance of her position.

He didn't realize his hand reached for her until his fingers brushed one of her curls. Dorian snatched his hand back and quickly turned on his heel.

Without a backward glance, he strode out onto the balcony and shifted. His wings spread as he jumped, launching himself into the air to head back to the swanky Dreagan residence just down the road from Alex.

Dorian landed on the roof and regrettably returned to the hated human form. He dropped his invisibility and walked naked through the door that led down to the apartment.

Dreagan owned the entire building, renting out thirty floors. But the top ten floors were all Dreagan. The top three were residences. Dorian chose the penthouse because he liked being as close to the clouds as he could get.

He made his way into the apartment and stood naked in the moonlight streaming in through the glass wall of the living room.

The lights of the city made it impossible to see the stars. It was another reason to hate New York. But at least he could bask in the glow of the moonlight.

He lowered himself to the floor and closed his eyes, his mind drifting. And to his utter horror, he found himself thinking about Alexandra Sheridan.

Chapter Four

Dorian. Who just had a first name?

There was Adele, Pink, Prince, and Eminem. There was even Fabio. But Dorian? No matter how hard Alex tried, she couldn't think why he wouldn't reveal his last name.

Even when she called the charity to ask how he paid, he simply gave them two names. Dorian. And Dreagan.

That had taken her aback. Everyone, whether they drank Scotch or not, knew Dreagan. It was one of the most recognizable brands of liquor around the world.

After learning that tidbit, it hadn't taken Alex long to make a connection between the two. Within minutes of doing a search on Dorian and Dreagan Industries, her cell phone rang.

Alex frowned when she saw the odd number. She'd placed enough international calls to recognize one when it popped up on her screen. Hesitantly, she answered the phone.

"Alexandra Sheridan, please," said a man with a deep Scottish accent similar to Dorian's.

"Speaking. How may I help you?"

"I'm Ryder calling from Dreagan Industries."

A chill went up Alex's spine. She couldn't help but think that somehow Ryder had known she was searching about Dorian. It was conspiracy theory crazy, but it was much more feasible than just coincidence.

"I wanted to let you know that Dorian is part of Dreagan," Ryder continued. "In case you were wondering about our connection."

"Why would you tell me that?" She had to know if he was spying on her.

Alex glanced at the camera on her laptop and realized that the cover she had on it had somehow fallen off. She quickly put her finger over the camera—just in case someone from Dreagan had hacked her computer.

Ryder chuckled. "I apologize. I can only imagine how all of this sounds. It was too late to place the call yesterday, otherwise Dreagan would have put your mind at ease last night. Dorian does things a wee bit different, and in today's world that puts some people off."

"In other words, he really wants to go on this date with me?" she said, frowning. She was perturbed, and she couldn't figure out why.

"Dreagan is a multi-billion dollar company, Miss Sheridan. We're all too aware of how important it is for people to know that they're dealing with those from Dreagan, and no' an imposter."

"Tell me Dorian's last name, then." She was going to get it one way or another.

There was a beat of silence. "He gave it, Miss Sheridan. It's Dreagan."

Dorian Dreagan. She repeated the name in her head several times, but it didn't sound right no matter how many times she said it. "I see."

"I willna take up more of your time. I hope you and Dorian have a pleasant time today."

"Thanks," she said, more out of habit than appreciation.

The call disconnected and she slammed her computer shut. No matter how she looked at it, something was definitely fishy about Dorian. If only she could figure out what it was.

She glanced at the time and groaned. Already she was running late. She loathed being tardy to anything—even a date she wasn't sure about.

And she hated that it was being called a date.

Through her shower and blow-drying her hair she couldn't stop thinking about Dorian and the call from Dreagan. Usually, she could figure out someone's angle or lie fairly quickly, but she was well and truly stumped.

She applied her makeup with more attention than she'd taken in years. And that only irritated her further. Why should she care what Dorian thought of her?

"Dorian Dreagan," she said with a snort. "Yeah, and I'm a monkey's uncle."

Still, she dressed, applied a bit of perfume to her inner wrists and behind her ears. Then she stood before her jewelry armoire.

There were diamonds, rubies, sapphires, and emeralds aplenty, but she shunned them except for formal events. Alex chose a simple gold necklace with small starfish her father had given her and gold bar stud earrings. She put on the gold T bar bracelet from Tiffany last.

A glance at her watch showed that she had only minutes to spare before she went down to her driver. After a look in the full-length mirror, Alex grabbed her purse and headed to the elevator.

With every floor the elevator descended, her nerves tightened until she was in knots. Then she stepped out of the elevator and walked to the doors, where her stomach dropped to her feet at the sight of Dorian leaning casually against her car.

There was no turning away because his gaze snagged hers through the glass doors. It was as if he'd known she was getting off the elevator.

She gave herself just a moment to admire him. Dorian had been dashing and entirely sexual in his kilt. Today he looked relaxed, but still oozed sex appeal, in dark jeans and a white button-down that showcased his extremely broad shoulders.

At this rate, she was beginning to think that there wasn't anything he could wear that didn't make him look mouthwateringly hot.

In the next heartbeat, she wondered what he'd look like if she stripped him of his clothes.

Her face heated and breathing became difficult. Why had her mind gone there?

Because you want a taste of him. Admit it, Alex. He sets your blood on fire.

Damn, but she hated when her subconscious was right. She did want a taste. And a lick.

And a touch.

Many, many touches, in fact.

It didn't help that he looked like he knew exactly how to make a woman scream in pleasure. It was his eyes. Those soft, sensual brown eyes.

Penetrating and *knowing*.

She had the inescapable feeling that he could see into her mind and determine her darkest, most wanton desires and bring them to life.

And she was going to spend the next few hours with him. Good God. What had she gotten herself into?

He pushed away from the vehicle, and she realized she'd been staring too long. Alex made her feet move toward him. She reached the doors and they were quickly opened by one of her bodyguards.

"Morning, Miss Alex," he said.

She glanced at Paul and smiled brightly. "Morning. Thank you and Tim again for last night."

"It's our pleasure, ma'am."

She'd liked Paul immediately. It was probably his Southern accent and manners, but he'd turned out to be one of her best bodyguards. After the attack the previous night, she was relieved to see him.

Her thoughts immediately went to the knife-wielding man, but her gaze was pulled away as someone demanded attention. A shiver went through her when she found Dorian standing before her, his eyes revealing nothing.

She quite liked his eyes. They were a mix of soft brown and amber encircled by a deeper brown bordering on onyx that made them impossible to miss.

His hair was once more pulled back at the base of his neck, and she had the urge to tug loose the leather tie that held the locks and see how long and thick his blond hair was.

"Ready?" Dorian asked and held out his arm.

"Good morning to you as well," she replied.

One side of his lips curved into a grin. "I didna think you cared about trivial pleasantries."

In fact, she hated them. Yep. He had to be in her mind. There was no other explanation. Alex sighed and took his arm.

As soon as she did, he said, "Did you sleep well, Alexandra?"

The sound of her name on his lips in that sin-inducing accent made her knees weak. And she made the mistake of looking at him. "I did. You?"

"I thought you might change your mind about today."

She thought it odd that he didn't answer her query, but she didn't push it. "When I give my word, you can trust it."

"It doesna hurt that you have your driver and four guards tagging along with us," Dorian said as he walked her to the Range Rover and helped her inside.

She'd wondered if he would bring that up. "It has nothing to do with you."

"You're safe with me, lass."

Her lips parted to answer, but there was no response other than the chills that raced over her skin. He couldn't know about the night before, but his words still had the desired effect of making her feel that no one would ever harm her when he was near. She got into the vehicle still dazed and looked at him.

Dorian climbed in beside her and shut the door before Paul could take his usual spot next to her. Instead, Paul got in the front seat with Yasser, her driver, while Tim, Leon, and Delroy took the Suburban to follow.

"So, what do you do?" she asked Dorian when he fell silent as they merged with the other cars.

He shrugged, but she saw how his hand had such a tight grip on the door handle that his knuckles were white. "I do whatever is needed."

"At Dreagan Industries?"

Dorian glanced at her and nodded. "Aye."

"Do you own it?"

"A part, aye."

That made her sit up straighter. "Do you actually help in the day-to-day running of the distillery?"

"I do whatever is needed, regardless of what that might be."

His answer wasn't exactly a reply, and she had a feeling it was all she was going to get. But that quickly left her mind when they turned left instead of right toward Central Park.

"Yasser, where are we going?"

He looked at her through the rearview mirror. "Dorian changed the plans."

"And you went with his idea?" she asked in shock.

"Because mine is better," Dorian replied.

Her head snapped to him. "I don't like change. I-"

"What I paid handsomely for was a few hours with you, Miss Sheridan," he interrupted. "The agreement never said that you get to choose the place. In fact, that is left up to me."

His taking command rankled her. "But I get to choose the time."

"Aye. And you did that."

She made decisions. She chose when and where and how she did things. Dorian strolling into her life and disrupting it wasn't something she wanted a part of.

But it was just for a few hours. So she would endure his company and then she'd never have to see him again.

Alex released a breath and faced forward while her anger simmered. The control she exerted was the only thing that was hers, the one thing she had to get her through each day. To have that taken from her was....

Her thoughts faded as they had pulled up before a building she knew well. Jacques wasn't just her favorite restaurant, but it was one with amazing views of the city and Central Park.

Maybe she had been hasty in her ire.

And perhaps it wouldn't hurt her to let someone have a tiny bit of the control she wielded so expertly.

Dorian was out of the vehicle and around the side to open her door before Paul could. Alex took Dorian's outstretched hand as she climbed from the SUV.

"Trust me," Dorian whispered.

She glanced at him in surprise, but then they were ushered into the building. To her shock she realized the entire restaurant was deserted.

"It's ours for the day," Dorian said. "I thought you might like the privacy."

"This is"—she looked around at all the empty tables—"perfect."

A lopsided grin filled Dorian's face, and she forgot to breathe. What was it about him that compelled her to agree with whatever he wanted? She didn't want to be with him, but she couldn't seem to stay away either.

Her attraction to him was so fierce and instantaneous that even now she was powerless to ignore it. And she wasn't sure she wanted to. Dorian set her off kilter most definitely, but there was something about his somewhat sullen, and definitely brooding, nature that appealed to her.

They were seated and wait staff filed in, led by the maître d' waiting to take their order. No one had ever done anything remotely like this for her before, and Alex found that she was happy Dorian had taken over.

Her idea of going to the park where there were other people around to fill in the silences now seemed stupid. Everyone would've stared and taken pictures. This was much better. More secluded.

And intimate.

She swallowed, suddenly all too aware that this was in fact a date. And sitting across from her was a handsome Scot who made her feel things she'd rather not experience—especially with him.

Because Dorian wasn't like any man she'd ever been around before. That both roused her and terrified her.

"I told you to trust me," Dorian said right before the pop of the champagne bottle.

Chapter Five

She was pleased.

And somehow, Dorian discovered that delighted him. Odd, given how much he hated humans. What was it about this particular female that made him want to do something for her?

Maybe it had been the attack the night before. Perhaps it had been the sight of her crying silently upon her balcony—alone. Whatever it was, he had woken that morning with the idea and made a call to Ryder, who'd discovered her favorite restaurant. After that, it was a matter of just another few calls to get what he wanted.

Dorian looked Alexandra over in her white sundress with the thin straps at her shoulders and the white sandals with the thick heels on her feet. It allowed him to see more of her amazing legs and the bright blue glittery nail polish on her toes.

Now that they were inside the restaurant without anyone else to overhear or bother them, he knew he'd made the right decision.

The only problem now was her four bodyguards, who were situated several steps behind her. Dorian looked at the one she had called Paul. The guard was tall, with blue eyes and dark hair—and his gaze often went to Alex.

It was obvious to Dorian that the bodyguard wanted Alex. What Dorian didn't know was if Alex felt the same. Since she didn't look Paul's way, she probably didn't.

"We're alone here," Dorian said.

Alex set down her champagne glass after taking a drink. She looked around and grinned. "That's pretty obvious."

"Perhaps we can dispense with your guards then?"

She hesitated, staring at him. Then she licked her lips. After another moment, she turned in her chair to address the men. "Why don't you wait at the doors?"

"I don't think that's wise," Paul said.

Tim, the shorter man with graying hair, quickly said, "As you wish."

The four of them walked away. When Alex turned around, Paul shot Dorian a look that said the mortal couldn't wait until he had Dorian alone.

And quite frankly, Dorian was looking forward to it. If the human wanted a fight, Dorian was definitely game. It wouldn't be a fair battle, but anything to rid him of his pent-up anger would be a relief. And if—

"Why this restaurant?"

It took him a moment to realize that Alex was speaking to him. He'd been so engrossed in his thoughts about what he'd do to the bodyguard that he forgot what he was supposed to be doing.

He shrugged. "I heard the food was good."

"You're taking a chance then," she said with a laugh.

To his shock, he smiled at the sound. "I am."

"I can't imagine that it was cheap to book the entire restaurant."

He shrugged again and finished off his champagne. When the waiter tried to refill it, Dorian put his hand over the glass. "Bring the bottle of Dreagan." Then he looked at Alex. "It's just money, and I wanted some time with you without others about."

"Thank you for this." She leaned forward and reached for her glass, then took a long drink.

Once the bottle of Scotch and a tumbler were set before him, Dorian poured some of the alcohol in the glass and asked, "So why the bodyguards?"

A change came over her at the question, like a castle gate slamming shut. "There was an incident."

"I gathered as much. Otherwise, why have four men protecting you? I understand if you doona wish to tell me." Dorian knew he could get the information from Ryder, but he would find out what had happened.

Alex stared at the golden liquid in her glass. "When I was eight years old someone tried to kidnap me from school for ransom to my parents. One of the other parents foiled the plan. When I was fourteen, there was a second attempt. That's when my parents hired a man to guard me at all times. Carlos went everywhere with me."

Dorian watched the way her shoulders hunched up to her ears and her forehead puckered in a frown. The words were hard for her, but it was the parts she was leaving out that were causing the reaction. He didn't press her for more. He got everything he needed just by watching and listening.

She blew out a breath and lifted her gaze to him. "There were times that Carlos was the only one between me and the slew of cameras with people trying to get a picture. There were a few times where people have tried to kill me simply because I come from money. There were at least ten death threats a week. He kept me safe through it all."

"Until?" Dorian asked, recognizing that there was more.

"Until five years ago when my boyfriend refused to accept that we were over and tried to shoot me. Carlos jumped between me and the bullet."

Dorian drank the Scotch and softly set the glass down. "That's when you hired four guards?"

"I tried doing without for awhile, but it soon became apparent that I couldn't go anywhere. So, yes, that's when I hired Paul and Tim. Leon and Delroy came on about six months later."

"That is no' a verra good life."

"Do you go out as you want?"

"Aye."

She raised a brow. "I told you something about myself. It's only fair you do the same."

Dorian leaned forward and refilled his glass, giving him time to think. He couldn't exactly tell her that he'd been sleeping for the last several million years.

"You don't like to talk about yourself," Alex said. She gave a nod. "I don't either. I think I'm pretty boring, actually. I don't do anything. I was just lucky enough to be born into a wealthy family."

"You're involved in charities," Dorian pointed out.

She lifted one shoulder in a shrug. "I just think I need to give back. I feel it's a responsibility. I don't do anything like you do."

"I do whatever Dreagan needs of me, and I always will. But I doona run the business. There are others for that."

"Is it a large company? I know how big the business is, but how many employees do you have?"

Dorian wasn't at all comfortable with this line of questioning. Then again, it was better than talking about himself. "Those we employ outside the family are few. We like to do the majority of things ourselves."

"How big is your family?"

"Big," he replied.

She crossed one long leg over the other. "I always heard that it wasn't wise to work with family."

"We wouldna have it any other way."

"It allows you to keep things private."

He grinned. "Aye, it does."

"I admit, I always hate the auction because I'm always afraid of who I'll have to spend a few hours with. But you intrigue me."

"Oh?" he asked with a raised brow.

She licked her lips and glanced away, her expression shuttered as her face turned red. "I... Well, usually men are doing whatever they can to get me into their beds."

Dorian realized she was embarrassed at the admission. And somehow he liked that. "How do you know I willna?"

Alex's hazel eyes briefly met his, her face flaming red.

"You're a beautiful woman. Is it any wonder men want you?"

She tucked her hair behind her ear, the pleasure of his words obvious in the way that her lips curved into a soft smile. "Yet most of those men want me only for my money."

"If they can no' see you for you, then they doona deserve you."

Alex blinked and leaned her head to the side, staring at him. "That's good advice."

He gave a nod and brought his glass to his lips, letting the smooth taste of the whisky slide down his throat.

The next few minutes were taken up with ordering food. Dorian couldn't stop looking at her. Alex wasn't anything like he'd imagined she would be. She was cautious, reserved, and vulnerable—though she tried valiantly to hide it. But he knew what to look for.

Paul saw it as well, which was one reason her bodyguard was so protective.

"Do you have anyone close to you?" she suddenly asked.

Dorian hesitated as he thought of the other Kings. "I used to, but I've kept to myself for a long time now."

"Why?" She then waved her hand, her face creased in regret. "I'm prying. Forget I asked."

"I lost someone verra close to me."

"I know all about loss." She uncrossed her legs and leaned forward to put her arms on the table. "My parents were killed in a plane crash when I was fifteen. My grandfather died of heart failure two years later, and my grandmother I lost six years ago."

Without thinking, Dorian reached over and put his hand atop hers. "I'm sorry."

And to his shock, he really was. She had suffered many difficulties, and he knew exactly how that felt. The fact that they had something in common, something that pushed him to actually like her, wasn't something he'd expected.

Their gazes locked for long moments.

"Thank you," she whispered.

Dorian spotted the arrival of the meal and removed his hand. They were silent as they ate, each absorbed in their food. He felt Alex's gaze on him and knew she wanted to ask who he had lost.

Once more she had shared, and she wanted him to do the same. If only he had something else to give her, but he didn't.

Finally, he set his fork down and leaned back.

"You don't have to tell me," Alex said. "I can see you still grieve deeply."

"I'll always mourn for her."

"Her. Oh," Alex murmured.

Dorian inhaled and softly blew it out. "My sister was murdered."

"Oh, God. That's awful. I'm so sorry." She reached out and placed a hand upon his arm in comfort. "Do you know who's responsible?"

"Aye."

"Have they been caught?"

He had to look away before his hatred consumed him. It rose swiftly, urging him to get retribution. It would be so easy. How could he answer her? He was sitting with one of the beings responsible for destroying everything, but he couldn't say that.

Memories of the mob of mortals attacking his sister filled his mind. He heard her screams of pain, saw her tears.

Suddenly, it was too much. He wanted to kill, to maim, and to wipe away every remnant of human beings from the face of the planet. With every fiber of his being he wanted things back to the way they were before the mortals arrived, when he had his family and his dragons.

He pulled his arm from her, suddenly unable to bear being near her. He thrust back his chair as he got to his feet to walk to the glass wall behind him and the view everyone in New York seemed to appreciate.

Everyone, that is, except him.

There was no way he could be here. He knew how important the artifact was, but he held too much rage, too much anger to be able to do what Con wanted. If only he could've gone with his plan where he wouldn't have to be around the mortals.

And he would after today. He just had to get through the rest of lunch, and then tonight he would take the object and return to Dreagan where he belonged.

A soft hand came to rest on his back between his shoulder blades and slowly slid to his arm as Alex moved to stand before him. Her eyes held a wealth of sadness that brought a rush of emotion that tightened his throat.

No matter how much he tried, he couldn't look away from her. He was trapped, ensnared by her eyes that held sympathy and understanding.

"I'm so sorry, Dorian," she whispered. "Is there anything I can do to help?"

He gave a shake of his head.

"I shouldn't have pried. Please forgive me. I'm just curious about you. I knew you didn't want to talk about it, and I pushed. It's one of my many faults."

He wanted to tell her that it was fine, but the words wouldn't come. To his surprise, she reached up and wrapped her arms around his neck, pressing her body against his.

The feel of her warmth and her softness undid him. His anger evaporated, promptly replaced with need that surged through him with such force that he shook with it.

How could his body betray him like this? With his enemy? She was his foe, wasn't she?

Dorian stopped thinking when her arms tightened and her breasts pressed against him. He inhaled deeply, pulling in the floral-citrus scent of perfume that didn't smell like a false scent, but rather a part of Alex.

His eyes closed, and for just a moment, he allowed himself to take comfort in the arms of a mortal, to forget the ever-present anger and just...be.

Chapter Six

A sigh left Alex when Dorian's arms finally came around her. His touch was light and hesitant, as if he wasn't sure he wanted to hold her.

But then his hands splayed upon her back and he pulled her close, holding on as if she were the only thing keeping him from shattering into a million pieces.

She knew that feeling all too well. So many nights she had lain in bed wishing she had someone to hold her as she struggled to pick up the broken pieces of her heart—and her life.

Even though she embraced Dorian to give him support, his hold was giving her comfort as well.

Alex never had anyone treat her with such reverence, with such fervor that it made her eyes prick with tears. Not once had Dorian flaunted his money, attempted to get her in bed, or assumed anything.

In short, it was the best day in a long, long time.

She closed her eyes and stood enfolded in his brawny embrace. For just a few moments, she didn't feel as if she had to stand against the world. No matter how briefly, it gave her battered soul a reprieve she hadn't realized she needed.

With each second that passed and they didn't break apart, her spirit soared, her heart strengthened. Was this what it was for someone to like her for *her* and not her money or standing in society?

She reluctantly leaned back, putting a few inches between them, and looked up into Dorian's soft brown eyes. His forehead was puckered in a small frown of consternation.

"You looked as if you needed a hug," she said.

He swallowed, never breaking eye contact. "No one has ever done that before."

"Then you've been around the wrong people."

"I isolated myself."

She let her hands slowly slide from his neck to his chest. "I remember doing that. It was getting out that made me see that the world moved on, indifferent and unsympathetic to my loss."

"How long did you hide away?"

Alex was all too aware that his arms were still around her, still holding her. And she liked it. A lot. "A few months. How about you?"

"Considerably longer."

That made her frown. "So you were close to your sister?"

"She was my only family. We were orphans, and she raised me. She sacrificed everything for me."

That made Alex's heart break even more. "There is nothing anyone can say that will dull the pain. I know loss well."

There was a flash of something in his eyes, but he blinked and it was gone. She wished she knew what it was. But she also realized that Dorian wasn't the type of man to spill his secrets easily.

If at all.

Perhaps that's why she wanted to know more about him. Of all the men she knew, not a single one of them was as interesting or disarming as Dorian. Not to mention, he was easily the most handsome man she had ever seen—and that was saying something.

It suddenly became impossible to look in his eyes. She glanced away, then focused on a button of his shirt. The silence was deafening, and she searched for something, anything to fill it.

When she glanced up, he was staring at her. The longer their bodies remained touching, the more aware she was of a growing—and insistent—longing for his touch.

And a hunger for his kiss.

Her breasts swelled, her nipples puckered. Thank goodness her strapless bra was padded, otherwise he'd feel how needy she was.

"Where are the others?" Dorian asked.

She was so relieved to have something to say that her shoulders sagged. Besides, if she kept thinking about all the things she wanted to do with his body, she might lean up and kiss him.

"I sent them out when you rose from the table. I knew you needed privacy."

"Why are you so kind?"

She was surprised at his question. "You ask that as if you expected something else."

"I did. In my experience, people are no' so pleasant."

"Like I said earlier, you've been around the wrong people. Surely you're not speaking of those at Dreagan."

He gave a single shake of his head.

"You quite confound me," she confessed. "When I look at you, I see someone who hasn't just experienced great pain, but someone who is incredibly worldly. I used to think I was experienced, but then I met you."

He quirked a blond brow. That one single action spoke volumes that words never could.

"I've traveled the world several times, but you've seen more," she continued. "Haven't you?"

His thumb slowly moved against her spine. "I suppose you could say that."

"I dreaded today, but now I want to stop time so you won't leave." She couldn't believe the words had left her mouth, but now that they were said, she was glad of it.

Surprise flickered in his eyes. "Then I'll stay. Tell me when you've had enough, and I'll leave."

"Just like that?"

One side of his lips lifted in the slightest of grins. "Aye, lass. Just like that."

"I don't suppose we can stand here in each other's arms."

"Why no'? Are you no' comfortable?"

She was mesmerized by his seductive voice, his enthralling eyes, and his arousing touch. Somehow, during their conversation he had pulled her closer. It had been so gradual she didn't realize it until her breasts were pressed against him.

"I didn't say that," she whispered.

He was going to kiss her. She could see it, feel it. And she wanted it. Desperately. She ached for it, yearned for it.

Then, he suddenly released her and took a step back. It was so unexpected that Alex found herself pitching forward so that he had to grab her. She was mortified. How could she have read that wrong? She'd seen the desire in his eyes, of that she was sure.

"What would you like to do?" Dorian asked after he'd steadied her.

Alex looked at the floor, wishing she hadn't made such a fool of herself. "Umm..."

And then she couldn't seem to talk. She didn't know where her brain or ability to speak had gone, but she wished they'd return. She didn't like whatever was happening to her, especially not with someone that she liked.

Damn. She did like him.

She should have recognized that when she said she didn't want the day to end, but it had been so long since she wanted to be with a man that it had taken her by surprise.

"We could have dessert," Dorian offered.

"Yes."

He escorted her back to their table, then asked, "What kind of dessert do you usually eat?"

Once more, her brain went blank.

His blond brow rose again. "Are you all right?"

"Yes. I don't normally eat sweets. Mostly because once I start, I can't stop. So I don't order them or stock anything in the house."

He leaned his head to the side after he filled his glass with more whisky. "What's wrong with eating something you enjoy?"

His question was so honest, so candid that she laughed. "The simple answer is to make sure I don't gain weight."

Dorian gave a shake of his head. "Who cares about that?"

"With every picture of me that is posted in the papers or social media, someone makes a comment about my hair, my makeup, my expression, or if I happen to be slouching, the size of my stomach."

"Tell them to bugger off."

Oh, if only she could. "It doesn't work that way."

"Sure it does. Besides, why do you care what others think?"

"I... Well, I don't know. For as long as I can remember, my parents would show me pictures of myself and tell me to stand straight or tell me what hair style and cut flattered me. They said if I was going to be photographed that I should look good."

"The way I see it, there is always going to be someone who isna happy with their life. They feel the need to take it out on others because they're jealous. You're no' just beautiful and an heiress, but have men lined up wanting you. To an outsider, you have it all."

She often told herself that, but it still didn't make the nasty comments easier to stomach. But really, she couldn't get past the fact that he'd called her beautiful.

"Why do you read their comments, anyway?" he asked.

She shrugged and accepted the menu of desserts from the waiter who appeared out of nowhere. "Probably because I know I shouldn't. But mostly because I can't seem to help myself. I guess I'm a glutton for punishment."

"Nay, lass. You want people to like you."

That was exactly what it was, but she had never told anyone, nor intended to admit it. Then Dorian spoke her secret aloud. "Yes."

He gave a nod to the menu. "I expect you to order at least one thing, but feel free to order everything."

Alex pressed her lips together as she smiled. This really was the best day. Dorian kept surprising her with his comments and the seemingly endless way he read her.

If only she knew more about him.

She ordered the lemon tart, and when Dorian's brow quirked, she found herself ordering the slice of turtle cheesecake as well.

Then he ordered the rest of the menu. Alex laughed, wishing the day could go on forever.

When Dorian raised the bottle of Dreagan in offering, she nodded. She wasn't much of a whisky drinker, but with him she felt the need to branch out and do things she wouldn't normally.

It felt good, freeing. And she really should do it more often.

"Tell me about Dreagan," she urged as she lifted the snifter to her nose and breathed in the heady fragrance.

He ignored her question and instead asked one of his own. "What do you smell?"

Alex took another deep inhale, letting the scents fill her. She closed her eyes and let the whisky envelop her. "There is a distinct woodiness about it. And wet, fallen leaves. Maybe a bit of apple and caramel. And sherry. Definitely sherry."

"Now taste it," he urged in a deep voice that sent shivers through her.

Without hesitation she brought the glass to her lips and let the liquid pass over her tongue and down her throat.

"What do you taste?"

She licked her lips and opened her eyes to find his gaze on her mouth. His eyes jerked upward, but it made her stomach quiver. "The sherry flavor I smelled, and apples. Also a hint of smokiness, which I really like. But it's the lingering woodsy flavor that I truly enjoy."

As she spoke, his eyes heated. "Do you want more?"

"Very much." And she wondered how the whisky would taste on his lips.

His mouth curved into a grin that made her heart skip a beat. The man truly had no idea of how the smallest things could affect her, and she was thankful for that.

Because if he knew, he could have her on her knees begging for his kiss in the next second.

Then again, if the day continued in this vein, she might do that on her own.

Chapter Seven

In all the things Constantine had kept Dorian abreast of, the food of the mortals wasn't one of them. As much as Dorian hated to admit it—and he really detested it—some of the human food was actually good.

Though he'd never tell them that.

When all fifteen desserts were set before them, he watched as Alex's gaze moved around the table trying to decide which to eat first. She had her fork in her hand, lifted and waiting.

As soon as she spotted the chocolate cake, she quickly speared a bite. To his dismay, his balls tightened with unexpected need when she closed her eyes and moaned once the sweet was in her mouth.

This was the second time that his traitorous body had reacted so to her. The first had been when she'd embraced him. No. Actually, it occurred once he wound his arms around her and felt her softness. Then she'd rested her head on his shoulder.

It had felt strange and unfamiliar, but too damn good.

That's what confused him. He wanted to hate her like he did the rest of humanity, but the more he was with her, the more he discovered that he actually *liked* Alex.

Her eyes opened as her lips curved into a sexy, satisfied grin. And all he could think about was he wanted that same look on her face after he pleasured her, her body so slack with indulgence that she couldn't move.

His mind came to a crashing halt. What the hell was wrong with him? Liking her was one thing. But...desiring her? That was quite another.

"Try this," she said, pushing the plate of chocolate cake toward him.

He glanced at the thick slice covered in chocolate icing, even between the four layers, and the lone strawberry on top—as if adding a fruit would make it healthier.

"Don't you like chocolate? Or is it cake you don't like?" she asked, a frown furrowing her brow.

Dorian shrugged. "I doona know."

Her eyes bugged out. "What do you mean you don't know?"

"I've no' eaten desserts before."

"You've got to be kidding," she said with a laugh. It died as she looked at him with shock. "You're not. How is that possible?"

Dorian was growing uncomfortable at her questions. He had no intention of telling her anything about his past, but now it looked as if he didn't have much of a choice. "I did tell you I isolated myself."

"From food?" she asked, astounded.

He shrugged, preferring not to reply.

She gave a little shake of her head and pushed the plate at him again. "Then you have to try it. Actually, you need to try everything. It wouldn't be fair to have such a glorious display and you not sample it all."

Oh, there was something he wanted to sample, but it wasn't the sweets before him.

Dorian grabbed his fork and leaned forward to cut into the dessert. She watched him as he put it in his mouth and chewed.

The explosion of flavor took him aback. It was sweet and decadent and entirely enjoyable. He went for a second bite, but Alex moved the plate and shoved another in its place.

For the next half hour, Dorian went through each of the desserts. Now he understood why Ryder always had a box of jelly donuts with him. Dorian really should have tried one of those, and he would remedy that once he was back at Dreagan.

"Well?" Alex asked excitedly after he swallowed the last sample. "Which is your favorite?"

He shrugged. "I like them all."

She rolled her eyes and huffed. "Oh, please. Everyone has a favorite. My grandmother's was cheesecake, but only the plain. Except during October, and then she wanted pumpkin cheesecake. I, personally, love all cheesecake."

"So that's your favorite?" he asked.

Alex grinned, her eyes crinkling as she shook her head. "Actually, I have an addiction to chocolate. Dark, milk, white—it doesn't matter. I love it all. And it's true love, too."

Before Dorian realized it, he was smiling. There was something about the way Alex talked. He saw the difference in her from last night where she was pleasant but reserved to today where she had lowered her walls and was herself. Amusing, generous, thoughtful, and spirited.

"Oh, my!" she exclaimed. "A true smile from you. You know, you should do that more. It makes your eyes shine with mischievousness. Which, I must say, looks good on you."

Did she have any idea how her words were affecting him? His cock was hard, need thundering through him. It was all he could do not to swipe the table clear of dishes and yank her on top before he covered her body with his to sink into her.

Unaware of his problem, she filled their tumblers with more whisky and sat back, the glass held in both her hands before her. "I'm waiting for your favorite. I've confessed many of my sins."

"Chocolate and cheesecake are sins?" he asked curiously.

She laughed and drew in a breath as she glanced out the window to the skyline behind him. "Things so delicious and decadent are definitely sins. But it feels so right to give in."

His blood heated at the throaty sound of her words. Whether she meant it or not, her words and tone were sexy and erotic, and they were doing quite a number on him.

"Come on," she said, giving him a seductive look. "Tell me your favorite. I can't leave here without knowing."

How could he resist that request? "I did like all of them. The chocolate is verra good with the cake, mousse, and chocolate and raspberry tart. I also really enjoyed the salted almond truffle tart. But I have to say that the lemon trifle was exceptional."

"So that's your favorite?" she asked.

Dorian shook his head and looked over at the display of bowls with their icy colored creations. "The gelato."

Once more Alex's eyes widened. "Really? Is there a certain flavor?"

"I like all six."

She threw back her head and laughed, a deep throaty laugh that went straight through his cock. "Oh, Dorian. There are hundreds of flavors. I know the perfect place to take you. It's in Little Italy, and they make the best gelato. Come on."

He let her take his hand and draw him out the door of the

restaurant where Paul and the other bodyguards awaited. Dorian saw the anger that filled Paul's face as Alex passed him with a bright smile that made her entire face light up.

Dorian didn't pull his hand free. She was walking ahead and turned to look over her shoulder at him. Her large curls swung around her as their eyes locked.

And his breath lodged in his throat.

He'd known from the first time he saw her picture that she was beautiful. But in that moment, with her eyes shining and laughter transforming her face, she took his breath away.

She pulled him along out of the elevators until they were both jogging to the cars. He worried that she might twist her ankles in the heels that she wore, but she didn't falter, not even when they hit uneven sidewalk.

He was conscious of how she didn't release his hand, not even when they climbed inside the backseat of the SUV. She was giddy as the guards got in and they drove, an excitement about her that he hadn't seen before.

It somehow rubbed off on him. He couldn't wait to reach their destination and see what kinds of flavors awaited. But only because she was so eager to show him.

As the vehicle wound its way through the busy streets of New York City, Alex pointed out sights and things that he should do while he was there. She talked nonstop, but it wasn't irritating. In fact, it was quite soothing.

There were a couple of places he was curious to check out and he made a mental note of them. And while he did look out the window, for the most part, his gaze was locked on something else.

A woman who surprised and charmed him. There were long stretches of time where he couldn't remember why he wanted to hate her. And then there was the ever present need that was quickly becoming a hunger he couldn't ignore.

From the flash of her sexy legs to her husky laugh to her curls that he longed to sink his fingers into, Alex had captivated him.

There was no other word for it. He didn't know how or when, but sometime during their outing, everything had changed.

"We're here," she said with a laugh and leaned over to open his door, pushing him out.

Dorian slid out and turned to help her, but she was already leading him to the shop. He glanced up at the sign as they went through the door. Then he stopped and stared at the array of colors and flavors before him.

Beside him, Alex was all smiles. "So. One of every flavor?"

"Oh, aye."

She tugged him to the counter and told the attendant before they found a table and waited. Dorian watched as the staff began scooping the gelato into containers. He didn't even care that Paul was openly glaring at him now.

Dorian would be gone the next day with the artifact in hand.

His good mood soured instantly. Shite. He'd forgotten that he planned to steal the object that night.

No matter how he tried, he couldn't bring back his mood from before. He attempted it once the first round of gelato was delivered and they sampled them.

Dorian loved the *caffé*, or coffee flavor, and ate the entire thing. In the next round, he discovered *stracciatella*, which was a soft vanilla flavor with chocolate drizzled on top that hardened and they stirred it together so it looked like little bits within the gelato.

The staff waited until the end to bring them nothing but a huge variety of chocolate gelato. Alex sat up straight, waiting to dive into the offering.

He let her taste them all first. Mostly because he loved watching her expressions. She truly was a chocoholic. There wasn't a flavor she turned away.

"I found it," she said and lifted a spoonful toward him.

He raised a brow. "What?"

"This is going to be your favorite. Trust me."

He looked at the nearly black gelato and smiled before opening his mouth. As soon as it hit his tongue, he knew she was right. It was amazing. The dark chocolate filled his mouth, surging with the soft, heavenly flavor.

"You like it," she replied with a grin.

"Verra much."

"But is it your favorite?"

He wiped his mouth with the napkin and swallowed the last bit. "I do believe it is."

"I knew it," she said with a laugh. "It's called *cioccolato fondente*. It means dark chocolate."

Alex waved over her guards and told them to get whatever they wanted. All but Paul partook in her offer. Dorian continued to ignore him while he and Alex finished the *cioccolato fondente*.

When it was finally gone, she dropped her spoon in the empty container and sat back with a sigh. "I'm stuffed, but it was so worth it for you to find your favorite."

"Why did it matter?"

She shrugged and looked down at her polished nails. "I guess because I wanted you to remember me and this day."

"I couldna forget you." And he meant it. Alexandra Sheridan was one mortal that would remain with him for the rest of eternity.

Her hazel eyes lifted and met his. "Really?"

"Aye, lass."

The soft smile on her lips told him that she was pleased with his answer.

"What shall we do now?" he asked.

She slowly sat up, her cool veneer back in place. "I think we should leave."

Dorian frowned as he looked around the shop that had been nearly empty when they arrived. More people had come in, and all were staring at Alex. Some with their phones out taking pictures.

He rose and stepped in front of Alex, glaring at the others. It took only a moment before they put down their mobile phones and looked away. That's when he turned and offered Alex his arm.

Paul and the others were waiting at the door. But once outside, there were men with large cameras snapping pictures as they left the shop. Alex ignored them, but he stared each of them down.

Inside the Rover, she glanced at him. "Thank you for your help. I'm sorry about all of that. It's why I don't go out much."

He understood. He wouldn't want to have cameras following his every move. The animated woman was gone, replaced by the reserved one—and he didn't like it.

"What shall we do now?"

Her head whipped around to him, surprise in her eyes. "Really?"

"You said you didna want the day to end. Have you changed your mind?"

Her smile was huge as she shook her head. "No."

"Then pick where we go."

"Home, Yasser," she told the driver.

Chapter Eight

The last person other than Meg or her bodyguards who had seen her place had been her ex. Alex was nervous for Dorian to be there.

What would he think? The fact that it mattered spoke volumes.

The security of her building was extreme, but Paul and Tim still went up to the penthouse first. Once they radioed down with the all clear, she and Dorian got in the elevator.

She fidgeted with her purse, her nerves strung so tight that she thought she might break. No matter how hard she thought back, she couldn't remember a time where she had ever been so anxious about anything.

Alex began to worry that she had made the wrong decision in bringing Dorian. What was there to do? She had a huge selection of movies and TV shows, but what if he didn't watch television?

Well, he didn't know what desserts were.

Exactly. What was up with that? Who didn't know about dessert? There was just something odd about that. Yet, it was also what made Dorian so damn appealing.

Sexy. He's damn sexy.

Ugh. Her subconscious really needed to shut up, because now all she could think about was taking him to her bedroom. After telling Dorian that all the men immediately hit on her, she was the one who wanted to rip his clothes off and lick every inch of him.

She'd felt the hard sinew of his body and knew just how firm and tight his body was. A body she ached to have on top of her, to feel him thrusting between her legs.

"You're blushing, lass."

Oh, God. She was. And the more she thought about his body, the hotter her face flamed.

Alex refused to look at Dorian. Nor did she know how to reply to his statement. Luckily, the elevator dinged and the doors opened to the penthouse.

She hurried out and tossed her purse on the entry table.

"I can leave."

His words brought her to a quick halt. Alex turned to him. "Only if you want to."

"You regret bringing me here," he said in his thick brogue. "I can see it in your face. And your eyes."

She looked away and took a deep breath. "I don't regret having you up. It's just been a really long time since I've had anyone other than those who work for me in my space. I'm...well, I'm nervous about what you'll think."

He closed the distance between them, walking slowly, his gaze locked on her. "This is your place. You get to decide what you like and doona like. Everyone else's opinion doesna matter."

"Yours does."

One brow rose as he tilted his head to the side. "Why?"

Alex glanced at the pictures, furniture, and decorations. "This place has been in my family for four generations. Everyone who has lived here has made their mark. I remodeled most of the space to suit me." She returned her gaze to him. "This isn't just my home. It's part of me."

"And you think if I doona like it, I willna like you."

"As silly as that sounds, yes." And it did sound crazy. "I know how lucky I am to be born into such a family. I have everything money can buy. But I don't have friends. It takes a lot for me to let anyone close enough to get to see this side of me."

Dorian walked to her and took her hand before leading her farther into the residence. The longer he remained quiet, the harder her stomach clenched.

She was attracted to Dorian, and that could be disastrous if he turned out to be anyone other than what he'd shown her. That's what frightened her. She really liked him, and she didn't want to be disappointed.

And she prayed he wasn't using her. That might very well break her forever.

They walked from the entry to the kitchen, dining, and living area.

They passed through the media room, her office, and down the hall to the spare bedrooms.

He halted before another hallway that led to her bedroom, but he turned the opposite direction toward the section of the penthouse that she hadn't wanted to update or remodel. It housed the collection of ancient artifacts.

At the doorway, Dorian stopped. "You didna remodel this part."

"No."

"The rest of the place has your touch in everything, but no' here."

She shook her head. "I thought about allowing museums to show off these beautiful pieces. It almost seems wrong to keep them away from others, but I'd never forgive myself if one of them was stolen. So I keep them here."

"Did you collect these?"

"It began with my great-great-great grandfather," she said as she walked among the artifacts. "He was in Wales on business and happened to find an ancient piece. Even then it was worth so much money that many tried to buy it from him. He had no clue what the artifact was, but he recognized its value. He returned to New York with it and had it analyzed."

"And?" Dorian asked.

Alex paused beside the gold necklace. "It is over six thousand years old. After he learned that, he began hunting for other such artifacts. It's an obsession that passed down through each generation." She held out her arms. "Everything you see here was amassed by all those before me."

"It's quite an impressive collection," Dorian said walking through the area, glancing at the objects through the cases.

She didn't bother to tell him that everything in the room would fetch three times what she already had in the bank.

Dorian faced her, his brown eyes regarding her. "I like seeing this side of you. And your place is simple and elegant. Timeless. Just as you are."

Her knees went all wobbly, as if her legs were made of Jell-O. And she nearly dropped down and begged him for a kiss.

Alex cleared her throat and turned around. As she walked from the back area, she slipped off her wedges and dangled them from her fingers, making her way to the kitchen.

She knew without looking that Dorian was behind her. She could feel him. His gaze was a hot caress over her skin that kept her heart beating double time and her blood rushing through her as desire pooled low in her belly.

"How about some coffee?" she asked. "Or would you rather tea? I have both."

"I doona know."

She whirled around as she reached the stove. "I'm beginning to believe you lived under a rock somewhere. Did you deprive yourself of everything?"

He shrugged, which wasn't an answer at all.

"Did you live in a monastery up in Nepal or something? I know they limit access to things."

"Something like that."

Again, not really an answer.

"How about I make coffee? If you don't like it, I'll make tea."

Dorian crossed his arms over his chest as he leaned against the doorframe. "Coffee will be fine."

Alex turned in a circle, trying to think of what to do before she reached for the mugs. Finally, her brain kicked in and she opened the fridge for milk. She said coffee, but in truth, she made lattes mostly.

Perhaps she should've told him that. Then again, anyone who didn't drink coffee or tea wouldn't know the difference.

She got everything ready and set it up. When she returned the milk to the refrigerator, she made the mistake of looking into Dorian's eyes.

Without thinking or second guessing herself, she quickly walked to him and rose up, placing her lips on his. Alex quickly stepped back, her chest heaving at doing something so atypical.

"What was that for?" Dorian asked in a soft voice that was deep and utterly sexy.

"The day was so great that I wanted to end it with something special."

"Is the day ending already?"

She shrugged and licked her lips. That's when she tasted him. The subtle, sultry flavor of dark chocolate gelato and whisky made her crave another taste.

Before she knew it, she rose up and kissed him again. Except this time, his arm snaked around her. In the next heartbeat, he had her against the fridge.

Her heart beat so loud she imagined he could hear it as well. She looked into his eyes that now blazed with such heat that she shivered.

"I'll give you a proper ending to the day," he murmured before slanting his mouth over hers.

Alex wrapped her arms around him, her fingers brushing the blond locks at his neck. She sighed as his tongue swept in her mouth before quickly leaving.

The tease was too much. She moaned, wanting more. And he delivered. Pressed between the appliance and his hard body, she felt every inch of him move as his tongue returned to tangle with hers.

It was no simple kiss. He claimed her mouth with such passion and hunger that she clung to him, needing more. With one long, hot kiss, she was his to do with as he wished. For however long he wanted her.

She sighed when she felt his arousal against her. Then his fingers sank into her hair. He wrapped the length around his hand and tugged her head back to expose her neck.

"Yes," she whispered.

He knew what she wanted and needed without having to be told. And it was doing glorious, amazing things to her body, which burned for him.

Suddenly, he turned her so that she faced the fridge. Her hands splayed upon the stainless steel that was cool to the touch. So at odds with her body, which was on fire.

Alex gasped in surprise and pleasure when his teeth clamped around the lobe of her ear, careful not to bite into her earring.

"Tell me to stop," he whispered against her neck.

Was he joking? That was exactly what she didn't want him to do.

"Tell me now, Alex. Otherwise, I'm carrying you to your bedroom. Then, I'm going to make love to you for so long that you willna be able to walk for a week."

"God, yes," she begged.

He spun her again and loomed over her, desire blazing in his eyes. "Last chance."

"If you stop now, I think I might die."

Alex forgot all about the coffee as he lifted her in his arms and strode to her bedroom.

Chapter Nine

Lust scorched his body hot as dragon fire. Dorian had attempted to ignore it, then Alex kissed him.

Twice.

Soft lips—and an even softer sigh—swiftly demolished whatever feeble attempt he'd endeavored to utilize in ignoring the sizzling need engulfing him.

The taste of her was more potent than wine, more seductive than an experienced courtesan. In fact, she was simple and surprisingly...exquisite.

The more they kissed, the hotter he became, the more he was reminded that it had been eons since his body had any kind of release. Even if he wanted to, he wouldn't be able to walk away from Alex now. He wanted her, needed her.

Craved her.

Dorian carried her into the bedroom and stopped before the bed. Slowly, he released her legs, allowing her amazing body to slide down his until she stood on her own feet.

He bunched the hem of her dress in his hands as he continued kissing her. While he wanted her clothes gone, he couldn't tear his mouth from hers. Because to be without her exotic, seductive kiss might just shatter the thin threads that held him together.

When she placed her hand on his chest and pushed, he stilled. His cock was so hard it ached, but he'd never forced a woman. And he wouldn't start now.

Then he caught sight of Alex's kiss-swollen lips, and his knees nearly buckled. He couldn't breathe, couldn't think about anything but being inside her, of feeling her slick heat surround him.

And hearing her call his name in pleasure.

His fingers fought to hold her as she stepped out of his arms. He hadn't known what he did wrong, but he would change it. All she had to do was tell him. He would fix whatever the problem was.

All thought came to a screeching halt when she reached behind her and pulled the zipper down. The white dress sagged on her shoulders before she tugged it over her hips to let it puddle at her feet.

His mouth went dry when he caught sight of the lacy white short slip over an even lacier bra and panty. He couldn't stop staring.

The lingerie highlighted her breasts, the indent of her waist, and the flare of her hips before teasing him with her glorious legs.

She then tugged the slip over her head and tossed it aside. With her chest heaving, she unhooked the bra and discarded it before bending to remove her panties. Only then did she stand straight, letting him look his fill from her pink-tipped breasts to the thin strip of blond curls between her legs—and every luscious bit in between.

Dorian's knees finally gave out. He reached out and pulled her to him, needing to hold her, to feel her warmth and softness.

He turned his head to the side and held her, unsure of the strange and unsettling feelings swirling through him. She tugged the leather holding his hair. He heard the soft thump as it landed on the rug right before her nails gently scraped his scalp and her fingers slid into his hair.

Whatever he'd intended, Dorian hadn't expected this. Nor could he fight it. Taking her as his lover wasn't smart, but he didn't care. He only knew how good it felt to have her in his arms. And he wanted more of it.

Didn't he deserve that? After everything?

He raised his head to look at Alex. Her hazel eyes swam with such yearning that it made his heart catch.

"I've never felt anything like this," she whispered. "What are you doing to me?"

"Making love to you," he said as he climbed to his feet and took her mouth.

* * * *

This was Heaven. Alex was sure of it.

Everything was right. There wasn't one bit of hesitation or worry.

She knew she was meant to be in Dorian's arms, and not even God himself could tear her out of them now.

Her fingers tightened in the cool, silky locks of his golden hair. With each tangle of his tongue against hers, she was sinking beneath the waves of desire, held securely by strong arms.

She usually worried about what her lovers thought of her body or how she was in bed. But the sight of the desire that literally blazed in Dorian's eyes right before he dropped to his knees had dispelled all of her insecurities.

Their kiss became frantic, each eager for the other. She heard a ripping and realized it was Dorian's shirt as he yanked it off. Somehow, they continued kissing through him removing his jeans. She wasn't sure how, but it didn't matter as long as she got more of his heady lips.

Then her gaze caught sight of something. She did a double take, their kissing at a halt as she stared at his left leg and focused on a tattoo that had a mix of red and black coloring.

But it was the drawing that made her pause.

The dragon was looking right at her, his gaze sharp and all-seeing. She took in the detail of the scales and the teeth before realizing that the tat made it appear as if the dragon was emerging from inside of Dorian's thigh.

The head of the beast, along with its arms and one wing, was visible. And she was disappointed not to see the rest of it. She lifted her face to Dorian to ask why that tattoo, but she became lost in his brown eyes.

His hands came up to cup her face while he turned her. Then she was on the bed. Her stomach quivered as she took in the glorious sight before her.

Utter perfection. Unreserved masculinity.

Absolute, unadulterated virility.

Chiseled abs, wide shoulders, thick arms, muscular legs, and a face that would make an angel sin.

He was a god. That was the only explanation. Somehow, he must have fallen from Mt. Olympus and ended up in New York, because there was no other explanation as to why someone who looked like him was alone.

Their eyes clashed, and her thoughts stopped. Dorian placed a knee on the bed and leaned over her, his hands braced on either side of her as his lips hovered over hers.

"I need this. I need you," she whispered.

Her eyes closed as he kissed first one eyelid and then the other before making his way down her face and neck. She held her breath when he reached her breasts, but he kissed between them to her navel.

She was so focused on his mouth that she wasn't paying attention to anything else. When his hands cupped her breasts, she gasped in surprise. It quickly turned into a moan as he rolled her hard nipples between his thumb and forefinger.

Suddenly, his lips clamped around one turgid peak. She rocked her hips against his leg wedged between hers as he began to tease her. His arousal pressed against her stomach and she held on to him with the tide of passion rising rapidly.

From one breast to the other his mouth moved. She was a tangled mess of need. And she wanted so very much more.

As if reading her mind, once more his lips traveled down her body. He didn't stop at her bellybutton this time. He kept going, gently moving her legs wider as he nestled between them.

She lifted her head, watching him. His gaze met hers as he spread her and bent to run his tongue along her sex.

A breathy moan passed her lips as her head dropped back on the bed, her fingers tangling in the duvet. Pleasure enveloped her as his tongue danced around her aching clit, bringing her ever closer to release.

So many times he brought her right to the edge and backed away, leaving her panting and yearning.

"Dorian," she begged.

In reply, he slid a finger inside her. She arched her back at the pleasure. He began to pump his finger inside her with aching slowness, tantalizing her with what she ached for.

With his tongue still flicking lightly across her swollen clit, he added a second finger. The climax was there, waiting to take her.

Alex tossed her head from side to side, the denial of what she needed making her entire body shake.

Suddenly, she jerked when Dorian suckled her clit into his mouth the same time he thrust his fingers deep inside her, touching her G-spot.

The orgasm came instantly. A scream lodged in her throat as her body convulsed from the raw, vigorous force of the pleasure that ran through her.

As the last vestiges of the climax left, she felt weighted down and lethargic. But all that vanished when she felt the blunt head of his cock at her entrance.

"Yes," she murmured and reached for him, wanting him deep within her immediately.

* * * *

The sight of Alex's pleasure was something he would never forget. It touched him in ways he hadn't been prepared for.

But her husky voice as he entered her made him fight not to thrust deep. She was incredibly tight, and he didn't want to hurt her.

He couldn't remember ever being so needy, so hungry to possess a female before. Her body stretched to accommodate him until all of him was inside her.

With their bodies locked together, the yearning that drove him only increased. It wasn't enough to see her pleasure or be inside her. He needed more. He needed it all.

Dorian began to move.

Slowly at first, building his tempo. She locked her legs around him, rising up to meet his thrusts.

In all his years, he had seen some beautiful things, but nothing compared to the sight of Alex's face flushed from her recent orgasm with her eyes staring hungrily up at him for more.

Their sweat-slicked bodies glided against each other as his thrusts went hard and deep. All he saw, all he felt—all that mattered—was the woman in his arms.

His own pleasure couldn't be held back. He buried himself deep and ground into her as he came. And to his surprise, he felt her clenching around him, her cries of release filling his ears.

When he could breathe easy again, he pulled out of her and rolled to the side, tugging her against him. He looked up at the ceiling when she rested her head on his chest. It took him a moment to realize what was different.

The heaviness that he'd carried since his sister's murder was lighter. It was still there, but not as suffocating as before.

There was a moment of guilt, but then Alex moved her hand to rest over his heart, and he was reminded of the ecstasy he'd just experienced. The moment was too pure, too amazing to let the past intrude—at least for the time being.

Dorian closed his eyes and simply allowed himself to be in the moment. He marveled at the fact that there was no hate in his heart, no anger. Just...contentment.

It had been so many eons since he'd experienced such an emotion that he nearly hadn't recognized it. Was this how the other Dragon Kings felt about their mates? If so, then he understood why so many had fallen in love.

The bliss lasted almost an hour before his thoughts turned to Dreagan and his brethren. That train of thought led him to recall why he was in New York in the first place. And just why he had sought out Alexandra.

His eyes opened once more, but this time it was regret that consumed him. He couldn't steal from Alex. Shite, the moment he heard her talk about the artifacts and how much they meant to her he'd had trouble reconciling his decision to steal it with how much he discovered he liked her.

Now, there was no way. None of that changed the fact that the Kings still needed the object. No matter how he looked at it, there was no way around what needed to happen.

That left him with only two options. Convince her to let him buy it. Or steal it. If he failed in the first attempt, she would know who took it.

He was so fucked.

Chapter Ten

Alex opened her eyes to find that it was dark outside. At almost the same instant, she realized she was alone in her bed.

She sat up and saw the pale pink rose on the pillow along with a folded piece of paper. Lifting the flower to her nose, she inhaled the fragrant bloom as she opened the note.

You looked too beautiful sleeping for me to wake you. See you soon.
Dorian

She smiled as she studied the bold, neat handwriting. Did anyone write notes anymore? Most sent texts or emails, which made this all the more special.

Alex leaned back against her headboard and sighed, a smile upon her lips. It was too bad the one person who had put it there was gone. She hated that she'd slept so deeply, but after having her body so satisfied, then curling up next to Dorian, she'd fallen instantly asleep.

It was the first time in a very long time that she had slept so soundly. She felt refreshed, revitalized. And not at all in the mood to go back to sleep.

Alex threw off the covers and carried both the note and flower into the bathroom. She put the rose in a small vase and filled it with water, then turned on her shower.

As the water heated, she walked naked into the kitchen to her purse and texted Meg to find Dorian's address. Today had been filled with so many firsts for her, and she was going to add another to the list by going to a man's house uninvited.

Twenty minutes later she stepped out of the shower and began to get ready. She opted for minimal makeup—just some smoky eyeliner, mascara, a hint of bronzer, and her favorite nude lipstick.

She pulled her hair atop her head and put it in a messy bun, which she usually reserved for days she didn't leave the house. But there was something about being around Dorian that made her want to have a more relaxed look.

It was thinking of him that had her reaching for jeans and a thin navy sweater that dipped low in the front. After donning a pair of brown booties, Alex studied herself in the mirror, liking the way the sweater showed just enough cleavage.

On her way through the kitchen, she went to reach for the small clutch she had carried earlier, but she paused. Too many years of matching everything was too deeply ingrained for her to disregard everything in one night.

She hurried back to her closet and chose another bag. After putting her things in it, she slung the purse over her shoulder. Then she jogged to the elevator, a smile on her face.

The doors opened on the bottom floor and she walked out to the lobby with only the security guard.

"Miss Sheridan," he said with a nod.

"Hi, Arthur. I forgot to call the guys," she said, reaching for her cell phone.

He held up his hand. "I'll do it."

"Thanks."

Alex walked to the doors and looked out the glass to the world right outside. People walked past, uncaring of who lived in the building. What would happen if she tried that?

She put her hand on the door, but an image of the man from the previous night trying to kill her stopped her cold.

It wasn't in her cards to have a life like others. In many ways she lived in a gilded cage. She hadn't minded it so much until today. She'd experienced something new with Dorian, and she wanted more of it.

Her phone dinged. Alex looked down to see a message from Meg with an address. A second later, the phone rang. She smiled when she saw Meg's name.

"Hey," Alex answered.

"You're going over there?"

The shock in Meg's voice made Alex laugh. "I am."

"You sound...happy."

Alex sighed. "I am."

"Oh, girl. You had sex. I can hear it in your voice, and I bet if I was there, I'd see it on your face."

Alex laughed again and felt her face flame. "You probably could."

"So he was good?" Meg asked.

"More than good."

"Shit. Really?"

Alex bit her lip as she thought of the way it had felt to have Dorian sink inside her. "Yeah."

"Then why the hell did he leave?" Meg asked angrily.

"Uh. Well, that was my fault. I fell asleep."

Meg grunted. "You haven't slept properly in three years. And after that kind of sex, you probably passed out."

"I think that's exactly what happened."

"He undoubtedly wanted another round with you."

Alex rolled her eyes. "Why do you think I'm going to see him?"

"About damn time you found someone who can screw your brains out and make you feel like the woman I know you are."

"I love you, too, Meg," Alex said.

"Uh, nope. You're not going to make me cry. Now get off the phone and go let that handsome Scot make you scream."

Alex giggled. "Bye."

"I want details tomorrow. Juicy details," Meg said right before she hung up.

Alex slipped her phone into her purse. When she looked up, Paul was walking toward her from the sidewalk where Yasser and the Range Rover waited.

"Everything all right?" her bodyguard asked.

She smiled at him. "Perfect."

He frowned, but held the door open for her, then ushered her to the SUV. She climbed into the backseat and gave the address to Yasser as Paul got in beside her.

Her driver flashed her a smile in the rearview mirror and pulled out into the traffic. It would have been just a few minutes' walk to Dorian's place, but in traffic it took nearly fifteen minutes.

She couldn't believe he lived so close to her. Though she hadn't bothered to ask where he stayed. As they approached the building, she looked at it with new eyes. The architecture was over a century old, but the building itself was in immaculate condition.

Since Dorian resided in the penthouse, she wondered if he owned the building. Not that it mattered. He could be penniless and she wouldn't care.

"Did either of you see Dorian when he came down earlier?" she asked the men.

There was a pause before Paul said, "I did."

"Did he say anything?" Alex didn't want to sound as if she were hunting for information, but that's exactly what she was doing.

Paul looked out the window. "All he said was that you were sleeping and shouldn't be interrupted."

Alex grinned. With just a few blocks to Dorian's, she wanted to jump out and run the rest of the way, but she knew Paul would be right beside her. So she remained inside the vehicle. Barely.

As soon as they reached the front of the building, Paul opened the door and waited for her.

"Are you sure about him?" the bodyguard asked.

Alex looked up into Paul's blue eyes. "I am."

"Perhaps I should come up with you."

"I'd rather you wait in the lobby."

She walked away before he could argue more. Thankfully, Paul didn't follow her to the elevator. There was a mix of nervousness and excitement in her belly as she rode to the top floor.

Except when the elevator opened it was to a foyer-like room with two doors. One was a single door off to her left atop a short set of stairs. The other were ornate wooden double doors with a dragon carved into each of them.

"How beautiful," she murmured.

She stared at the dragon thinking of Dorian's tattoo. Now she realized why she had been able to get on the elevator with no doorman in the lobby. Alex ran her hand over her thigh and walked to the door, her boots silent on the beautiful rug she hadn't noticed until then.

Her heart hammered with anxiety as she rang the bell. Then she waited for Dorian to answer. The seconds turned to minutes. She rang the doorbell again, though now she worried that he might be out. She hadn't bothered to call him to see if he was in. She'd wanted it to be a surprise.

After five minutes, she turned to leave when she heard the sound of wind whistling. She followed the sound to the other door atop the steps.

She walked up them, and as she neared, she realized the door was cracked open.

Alex slowly pushed open the metal door to peer around. Since the only one who had access to the roof was Dorian, she thought he might have a rooftop area like so many did.

She opened the door and stepped out to the roof. The force of the wind slammed into her just as she realized there was nothing to bring him up here. No sitting area, no garden. Nothing.

She crossed her arms over her chest and shuddered against the cool temperatures. Just as she contemplated returning inside, she realized that, while she might need furniture to bring her to the roof, Dorian might not. Perhaps he liked things just the way they were—barren.

She ventured forward, her gaze sweeping the area for a glimpse of him. Alex walked one direction and then the other. Just as she was giving up, she spotted Dorian standing on the edge of the roof.

She parted her lips to shout his name and get him off the ledge, but he vanished. Replaced by an enormous dragon with deep coral scales.

Before she could process that terrifying imagine, the creature spread its massive bat-like wings in the same reddish shade of orange. The next instant, it was gone.

Alex stood frozen, unsure if she had gone crazy, or had she really just seen a dragon? She took a step back and shivered as she heard the unmistakable sound of wings flapping.

Shock and fear flooded her, threatening to choke her and silence the scream that welled up. She didn't doubt what she'd seen, didn't question her sanity. The proof had been just a few dozen feet from her.

Without looking back, she turned and raced down the stairs to the elevator. She punched the down arrow repeatedly, hoping that would get it there faster.

Finally, the doors opened and she rushed inside, jabbing at the lobby button to hurry things along. Once the elevator was descending, she leaned against the wall and closed her eyes.

She knew it had been Dorian up there. She'd recognized his long, blond hair. But the dragon? That couldn't be real. Dragons didn't exist.

Alex was out of the elevator before the doors opened fully. She said nothing to Paul as she headed to the SUV, despite his worried look. Neither man commented on her silence as they drove. At her building, she couldn't get to the security of her home fast enough.

But as she stood looking out the windows at her balcony, she realized that a dragon could easily fly overhead. For that matter, it could land on her terrace.

Alex took a step back, suddenly terrified.

"Dragons aren't real," she said.

And people didn't shift into other beings, no matter how many books and shows said otherwise. She knew what was real and what wasn't.

How didn't he know about desserts? What about the coffee and tea?

"He's Scottish. Everyone drinks tea there," she said.

There's also the little matter of how he knew where your room was.

Alex stilled, her heart thumping. Her bedroom was the only place she hadn't shown Dorian. And while he might know which direction, her hallway had several doors. How had he known which one to take?

Chapter Eleven

Flying cleared his head. Usually.

But this time, when Dorian returned to his penthouse, he was still as confused as when he'd left Alex's. He knew the easiest, simplest thing would be for him to use his magic, return to her home, and steal the artifact.

Yet, he couldn't. No matter how many times he told himself to do it.

Dorian stood on the roof back in his human form and watched the sun rise. While it was a magnificent sight, moonrise was his favorite time.

Not because the darkness hid all manner of sins, but because it allowed the stars to show through the night sky and the moon to shed its light upon the earth. The sun might allow others to see all the colors that abounded on the realm.

But moonlight gave everything an ethereal glow. There were plants and animals that didn't come alive until the otherworldly light fell upon the land. So many missed out on the beauty because they feared the night.

Aye, there were monsters in the dark. Yet, they were also in the light, standing right beside the mortals. And they never knew it.

Dorian turned away from the bright ball of light rising in the horizon and made his way to the door to return to the flat. He had taken one step down the stairs when he came to a halt and frowned.

He drew in a deep breath. This time he knew for sure what he'd caught a whiff of—perfume. It wasn't just any scent. It was Alex's.

Backing up a step, Dorian used his enhanced senses and sought out the aroma that was Alex's alone. Shock reverberated through him when he realized that she had stood on the roof. And recently.

The stark, rancid odors of the city combined with the wind prevented him from discerning where she had been on the rooftop, but he had a pretty good idea of what she might have seen.

Always before he shifted, he made sure to use his magic and turn invisible. Last night had been different. He'd wanted to see if anyone noticed him. The humans were too busy with their insignificant lives to bother realizing that a dragon stood on the rooftop.

If anyone had, Dorian would've heard about it because it would've been all over the thing mortals called social media. Ever since the video the Dark Fae leaked of the Kings shifting and fighting Fae, there had been a rush for the humans to find anything and everything to do with dragons.

Dorian had been defiant because he'd been only thinking of himself, not his brethren back at Dreagan. He knew better, but his anger toward the mortals clouded his thinking sometimes.

He turned on his heel and went back inside the building. He then stood on the stairs and let the door shut behind him. With his eyes closed, he focused everything on the scents around him.

It was easy to pick out Alex's. He was attuned to her—had been since he first saw her at the charity event. But it went to another level after he took her as his lover.

He shifted through the smells and focused on everything that was hers. From her excitement to her nervousness to...her fear.

His eyes flew open. Without a doubt, he knew she'd seen him. Slowly, he walked to the double doors of the penthouse and pushed his dragon magic into the entry to unlock the spells. After he stepped inside and shut the door, he stopped.

He didn't know what his next move should be. The logical choice would be to forget her. No one would ever believe her, and she had no business learning of his secrets, regardless if she had seen him or not.

Then he thought of her smile and the warmth in her hazel eyes as she gazed up at him while they made love.

For reasons he couldn't explain or comprehend, he refused to walk away from her. Which brought on a whole slew of other problems for him.

No doubt she'd told Paul and the others to refuse him entry. In order to see her, he'd have to fly to her. While that seemed the easiest solution, he didn't think he could stand to see the terror in her eyes.

Not after she had looked at him with such adoration.

Which brought him back to letting her go. Dorian found a pair of jeans and put them on before he squeezed the bridge of his nose with his thumb and forefinger. Flashes of the day before kept running through his mind. It had been a good day.

He hadn't realized how desperately he'd needed one until Alex had gifted him with it. His intention had been to get close to her to attain the artifact. All the while, she had been enjoying his company.

The fact that he had treated her as the mortals had acted toward his sister sickened him. The very beings he loathed with every fiber of his being. He was disgusted with himself and the entire situation.

Things had been so uncomplicated when he hadn't liked her, when he hadn't yearned to have her in his arms.

His head snapped up at the pounding on his door. No one came to see him. Not until Alex. He strode toward the entry, hoping that it might be her, but as he neared, his hearing picked up the sounds of harsh breathing.

A man.

He opened the door and looked into Paul's blue eyes. The bodyguard's face was set in harsh lines, a muscle ticking in his jaw as his gaze shot daggers at Dorian.

"What did you say to her?" Paul demanded.

Dorian raised a brow. "Whatever did or didna occur between me and Alex is none of your concern."

"You didn't see her," Paul said and took a menacing step forward.

Dorian glared at the mortal. "Careful. You doona know what you're about to tangle with."

"I could say the same of you." Disgust filled Paul's face as he looked Dorian up and down. "You're not fit to lick her feet."

"And you're jealous of the fact that she's with me and no' you. Isna it bad to fall in love with your employer?"

Paul snorted in derision. "You don't know anything."

"I've got eyes. I see what she hasna. Perhaps you should learn your place."

The guard moved his jacket back to show the gun holstered. "Let me just remind you of who I am."

Wrath swirled through Dorian in a violent storm. This was exactly what he needed. A fight. It would feel good to hit a mortal—especially one who lusted after Alex.

"If you're going to threaten someone, then do it properly," Dorian said. He jerked his chin to the pistol. "Take it out and point it at me."

Fury sparked in Paul's eyes. "If I take my gun out, I use it."

"Then what are you waiting for? An invitation?"

"That's your problem," Paul stated in revulsion. "You don't fear anything."

Dorian held the human's gaze, his skin sizzling with the need to smash his fist into something. "Carry through with your threat or leave. But do something."

Paul closed his suit jacket. "Leave Alex alone. She doesn't need you."

Of that they could agree, but Dorian wouldn't admit anything to the human's face. He remained in his spot until the elevators closed and brought Paul back to the lobby. Only then did Dorian softly close the door.

The only problem was that he was now wound up and in need of taking it out on someone. If he didn't release his anger somehow, things could go horribly wrong.

He turned and leaned back against the wood. When he was younger, nothing had ever angered him. It took so much to get him mad, but even then, he never held onto it. All that changed with the murder of his sister. Ever since, he hadn't been able to shake the fury that consumed him.

The only one who had given him a measure of peace in millions of years was Alex. And he had lost her. Though, if he were honest with himself, he'd never had her.

Desire might have ruled him, but their worlds were too different. And the fact that she ran after seeing him in his true form was all the answer he needed.

He felt a push in his head as he heard his name. Opening the mental link, he answered the King of Dragon Kings' call. *"Con."*

"How are things?"

Dorian frowned. *"Surely you've more important things to do than check on me. Or are you afraid I've killed some humans?"*

There was a beat of silence before Con said, *"If I didna think you could complete this mission, I wouldna have sent you. However, I also know how hard this is for you. I shouldna have sent you alone. You've been asleep* a long time, old friend. All this is a lot to take in."

"Aye, it is."

"Then return home. We'll figure out another way to get the artifact."

Dorian ran a hand down his face and sighed. "I can do this."

"We all have our limits, Dorian. Even me."

"Have you reached yours?"

Con was silent a long time. "I have responsibilities that outweigh what I might want."

Which meant that Con had been at his limit for some time. So many Kings had been dealing with the constant fight of the Dark Fae, Mikkel—Ulrik's uncle who had tried to reveal the Kings to the world— and the new enemy. All while Dorian slept.

Just because he couldn't handle his sister's death. How bloody selfish was he? Every one of the Kings had lost something during the war. What made his grief any worse than theirs?

"I've hidden for too long," Dorian said. "It's past time I stood with the rest of you against our enemies."

"There's the Dorian I remember. Glad to have you back."

Dorian grimaced. "You might no' say that once you hear what's happened."

"Then you better tell me."

For the next ten minutes Dorian relayed everything to Con, including taking Alex to bed.

"We've dealt with worse situations." Con sighed. "What's your plan now?"

"The verra thing I wanted to do when I first came. Steal it."

"Hmm. And the peace she gave you? You would throw that away?"

Dorian was taken aback. "You want me to go to her?"

"I didna say that. I'm merely pointing out that you had contentment, which deserted you some time ago. And if you steal the artifact now, she'll hate you until the day she dies."

"She ran, Con. Her fear was so strong I could still smell it. We saw what a human's fear did to Ulrik. I've no wish to put myself there."

Con blew out a long breath. "I've never made my worry about the Kings taking mates a secret, but there is something to be said for the happiness the others have found. We all deserve that."

"There is more at stake here than me."

"Then you better take care of the thread of anger I hear in your voice before you steal the artifact. That rage has festered in you long enough."

"I know."

"It's no' like you can fight a mortal," Con added. *"I'll always have your back, Dorian."*

The link was cut off, Con's words echoing in his head long after.

Chapter Twelve

Nothing made sense now. Alex sat in a corner among the ancient artifacts with her legs drawn up to her chest and her arms wrapped around them.

She'd been there since returning from Dorian's. No matter how she tried to reason and reconcile what she'd seen, she couldn't. She wanted answers, but in order to do that, she would have to confront Dorian. And she didn't think she could.

"Alex?"

She turned her head toward the door when Meg's voice reached her. "Back here."

The sound of heels moving from floor to rug to floor again brought her assistant closer. "Have I got a story for you. I would've been here thirty minutes earlier, but I got to reading more of that blog, the *(Mis)Adventures of a Dating Failure*. I need to find out who this woman is. She's my soul sister. It's either that or she's been spying on me with my dates."

Alex leaned her head back. At one time, she and Meg had tried to find out who the blogger was, but they couldn't even locate what country she was in. It didn't help that the blogger had the site set up so that it automatically translated into the language of whatever country you were in.

The footsteps halted, as did Meg's words. "Alex?"

The worry in her friend's tone made her sigh. "I'm right here."

Meg leaned to the side to look around one of the pillars, her long black hair pulled back in a slick ponytail. "Uh oh. Last night you were on top of the world. Now it looks like you're carrying its entire weight."

Alex shrugged. She couldn't exactly tell Meg what she'd seen.

Her assistant walked over, kicked off her Jimmy Choo heels and sat beside her. "You're in jeans. You never wear jeans outside of the apartment."

"I know."

"Dorian got you to do that?" Meg pressed, hopeful.

Alex released her legs and let them stretch out before her. "He didn't ask. It's how he made he feel. Like things were easy and undemanding. I liked that he was in jeans yesterday."

"So what happened when you went to see him? Because I'm guessing it wasn't good since you're here and not in his bed."

Alex drew in a deep breath and blew it out. "He's not who I thought he was."

"Hmm," Meg said as she crossed her arms over her chest. "Since we didn't know very much about him, that's a feat in itself."

"He was so...real, yesterday. I've never been so relaxed around someone before."

Meg looked at her, a thin black brow raised. "Or slept with them on the first date."

Alex closed her eyes and shook her head. "He was amazing. I felt beautiful and cherished and needed. And the pleasure, Meg," she said, opening her eyes and looking at her friend. "It was unlike anything I've ever experienced."

"Well, to be honest, you don't have much of that, but..." Meg said when Alex opened her mouth. "The fact that you're talking like this must mean Dorian is some kind of sex god or something."

"Funny, I actually thought he might be just that. Between that amazing body and his skills in bed, he's no ordinary man."

Meg sighed long and loud. "Honey, men like that are as rare as the perfect diamond. If you find one, don't let him go."

"That's easy for you to say."

"What happened?"

Alex looked away, still unsure about telling her.

Meg's face took on the *oh, no, you didn't* look. "Was he with another woman?"

"That would be easier to explain."

"Did he refuse to see you? Was it a one-night stand?"

"I don't know."

Her assistant threw up her hands in defeat and let them fall to her lap. "I'm at a loss, then."

Alex briefly squeezed her eyes shut. "You won't believe me."

"You're the only one who has never lied to me. If I'm going to believe anyone, it's you."

Alex met Meg's dark gaze. Her friend nodded, and Alex took a deep breath. "Remember that I warned you."

"Just tell me already," Meg pushed as she turned to face her.

"He wasn't in his apartment. I saw stairs that led up to the roof, so I went up, thinking he might be there."

Meg nodded in agreement. "I'd have done the same thing."

"I didn't find him at first. When I did, he was standing on the ledge."

With eyes widened, Meg reached for her phone. "I didn't hear the news this morning because of the blog. Did he jump?"

Alex put her hand over Meg's. "No. It's worse than that."

Meg shot her a dubious look. "What's worse than death?"

"He shifted into a dragon." Alex said it in a rush before she changed her mind. Then she waited for Meg to tell her she was crazy and laugh.

Except Meg didn't.

Her assistant's face went slack.

Alex shifted toward her, gently shaking her. "Meg? Are you all right?"

Meg blinked, opening and shutting her mouth several times.

"You're scaring me," Alex told her.

Meg cleared her throat and climbed to her feet. "I need something to drink."

Alex scrambled to her feet and hurriedly followed her into the kitchen. "It's not even nine in the morning," she said when Meg opened a bottle of wine and brought it to her lips, totally disregarding a glass.

"You're not making me feel better about telling you," Alex said, growing more anxious by the moment.

Meg put down the bottle and took several deep breaths before she faced Alex. "Do you remember months and months ago me telling you about the video everyone was talking about?"

Alex shrugged. "No."

"It was from an anonymous source showing men shifting into dragons and dragons shifting into men all while they were fighting some other men who threw bubbles of magic at them."

Alex's knees threatened to buckle, so she hastily sat on a barstool. "Did I see it?"

"You wouldn't look at it."

"Then do you still have it?"

Meg shook her head. "Someone with some serious power erased every single shred of evidence of it. They went into The Cloud, Alex, and wiped it. Once something is in The Cloud, there's no getting it back, and yet someone did."

"He didn't know what desserts were."

Meg's brows shot up as she leaned her forearms on the island and cocked her head. "You lost me."

"Dorian. He'd never tasted dessert before yesterday. And he had never tasted coffee or tea."

Meg's lips twisted. "I could give him a pass on the coffee or tea, but desserts? Nope. That I don't understand."

"Do you think that video was real?"

"That was the argument. Some believed it to be a hoax, but others were convinced it was real. And they even suggested a place." Meg's face wrinkled as she winced. "And I can't believe I even forgot about this. It should have clicked the other night."

"Meg," Alex urged. "Where was the place?"

"Dreagan."

It was a good thing Alex was sitting down, because her knees would have given out. "Oh shit."

"Alex, if that video was real, and it was those at Dreagan who made sure they removed it, and Dorian is from Dreagan, then you definitely saw what you saw."

She sat back, letting that sink in.

"What did he look like?" Meg asked. "Did he try to hurt you? I can't believe I didn't think to ask that before."

"He never saw me," Alex answered absently. "And he was massive. I've never seen an animal so big before."

"All the dragons in the video were different colors. I do remember that. What was he?"

"Coral. I was too frightened to realize it then, but the color was quite splendid. Then he went invisible and flew off."

"Shut the front door!" Meg exclaimed as she straightened. She turned and took another long drink of wine. She smacked her lips and put a hand to her chest when she finished. "That would explain why no one reported seeing a dragon. So, you're telling me he could be in this room now and we wouldn't know it?"

Alex nodded.

Both were silent for a long moment as they each got lost in their thoughts. All Alex could think about was that she had made love to a dragon. A handsome, amazing, seductive dragon.

And she'd do it again even though she was still scared of him. Because the way she felt in Dorian's arms was better than anything else.

"He came to New York for a reason," Meg suddenly said. "He made it obvious at the event when he bid on you that he wanted you. As beautiful as you are, I don't think it was just to get you in his bed."

Alex grunted. "Trust me when I say he could have anyone."

"Yep. He sure could," Meg agreed. She shrugged when Alex shot her a dark look. "What? I'm human and he is seriously hot. I'd do him."

She couldn't fault Meg for that. "Why me, though? There are plenty of other heiresses."

"Maybe because you don't date guys?"

Alex rolled her eyes. "Dorian didn't know desserts or coffee. I sincerely doubt he cared about my social life."

"Then what else is there?"

Then it hit her. Alex rose and made her way to the museum, Meg on her heels. "There's something here he wants."

Meg blew out a breath as she crossed her arms over her chest. "But which one? And if that was the case and he can turn invisible, why hasn't he taken it? He was here yesterday with you asleep. He could have stolen anything he wanted."

But he hadn't. There wasn't anything missing.

Alex faced Meg. "I've got to see him."

As she was turning away, Meg grabbed her shoulders and pushed her toward the bedroom. "Tidy yourself up first."

"Right."

Fifteen minutes later, Alex had washed her face, brushed her teeth, applied new makeup just like the night before, and changed into her only other pair of jeans and a white shirt with a black leather moto jacket and black knee-high boots.

"Ready?" Meg asked.

Alex shook her head. "No. I'm scared."

"He made love to you," Meg said with a soft smile. "If Dorian wanted to hurt you, he easily could have. Instead, he gave you pleasure.

Think about that."

"Good point. Let's go."

She wanted Meg with her on the ride to Dorian's. Alex barely noticed the photographers outside her place or the ones following her. Her mind was focused on other things.

Once she reached Dorian's building, Meg and Paul walked her inside. Alex somehow made it to the elevator and punched the button for the top floor.

This time she reached it twice as fast as the previous night. Her nerves were tightened in a painful knot in her gut. The doors of the elevator opened, but she didn't get out. It wasn't until they began to close that she hurriedly stepped forward to stop them.

The doors hit her hand and slid open again. Alex really hoped she knew what she was doing. She shook everywhere as she made her way to the beautiful wooden doors and pressed the bell.

Chapter Thirteen

The rage was blinding, the resentment consuming.

Dorian's hate for the mortals mixed with his disappointment over Alex—not that he blamed her. He had seen firsthand how humans feared them. Even when the Kings shifted territories to give them a place to live instead of killing them.

How could they have been so wrong about the mortals? How could one act of kindness by allowing the humans to remain on this realm bring about the Kings' downfall?

The fact that he couldn't answer those questions only made him more violent. Con was right. He needed to blow off steam. Unfortunately, Dorian couldn't attack the very ones responsible. Nor did he have anyone to spar against. He'd have to wait until he returned to Dreagan.

And that would be tonight.

As much as he detested the position he was in, he was going to steal the artifact from Alex that night and fly back to Scotland to join his brethren and figure out their next course of action against their new enemies.

The soft chimes of the doorbell interrupted his thoughts. In the mood he was in, the last thing Dorian needed to do was answer the door and find Paul again. Because Dorian knew he wouldn't be able to hold back his anger.

It was remaining in the flat that was driving him daft. He had nothing to do—and only memories of Alex that were on repeat. Not a good combination for a Dragon King who was barely holding on to his control.

The doorbell rang again. Dorian strode to it. Just as he yanked it open, he caught a whiff of perfume that he knew well, and all his anger evaporated by the time his gaze landed on Alex.

Her blond curls were piled atop her head with a few strands teasing her neck. His gaze raked down her body, hunger pounding through him to claim her again, to taste her again.

His balls tightened when he saw the way the jeans molded to her long legs. As his gaze worked its way back up her body, he saw how her fingers dug into her purse nervously.

By the time he looked back into her hazel eyes, he steeled himself for whatever she had to say. The fact that she had returned said a lot, however.

Still, Dorian decided to let her choose if she would reveal what she'd seen. He bowed his head. "Good morn."

"Morning," she said with a small smile that quickly vanished.

He stepped back and widened the door. "Would you like to come in?"

She looked past him, hesitating. Finally, she moved into the flat. He softly closed the door and watched the way her gaze scanned the place.

Dorian paid no attention to the furnishings or the décor of the flat. It was a place to stay, to hide while on his mission. That's all that mattered to him.

Or it had. Now, as he watched Alex inspect the penthouse, he very much wanted to know her thoughts. The Dragon Kings had homes in all major cities—sometimes more than one house. None of the Kings owned them individually, and yet the residences belonged to all of them to use as needed.

"I didna know you were aware of where I lived," he said, needing to break the silence.

Alex turned her head to him. "Money can get you pretty much anything you want."

Dorian searched for something else to say, but he was at a loss. He wanted to know why she was there. But mostly he wanted to know what she'd seen the night before. Those questions, however, remained unspoken.

Because he knew if he uttered them, he would likely get the answers he dreaded. Then she would be gone. So he was dragging out the inevitable, just to be near her for a little longer.

"Why didn't you know about desserts or coffee?" she suddenly asked.

Dorian frowned at the unexpected question. "I told you, I removed myself from everything."

"But what does that mean exactly?" she pressed. Alex blew out a breath and set her purse on a side table by the sofa. "Who are you?"

So here it was. The question she came to learn the answer to. "I told you."

"You told me next to nothing."

He looked toward the windows and the city. "I told you of my sister, which is something I doona share."

There were only ten steps separating them, but it felt like a continent to Dorian. How did he bridge that gap? Or did he even try?

"And I thank you for that," she said. "That was the only real thing you told me about yourself. What are you hiding?"

Dorian returned his gaze to her and lifted a brow. Having her near and not being able to hold her was worse than when he thought he'd never see her again. For his sake, and hers, he needed to end whatever this conversation was.

"You tell me, since you were here last night," he stated.

Her lips parted in surprise as she took a little step back.

He snorted and shook his head. "You ran away only to return. Why?"

"I need answers."

"You're no' going to get them."

The fear in her hazel eyes was replaced with ire. "Because I don't deserve them?"

"Because you're better off no' knowing."

She crossed her arms over her chest and stuck a hip out, a move that Dorian learned was one that meant the female was just getting started.

The smile Alex gave him was anything but kind. "Which of the artifacts did you come for?"

Dorian should've realized that she would figure it out. Alex was smart, which most people didn't give her credit for. Still, he wouldn't answer her.

She blinked rapidly as her chest began to heave. Her arms dropped and she hurriedly looked away as her face crumpled. "I thought you were different. I didn't think you would use me, but you're just like the others."

"I'm no'."

"You are!" she shouted, the anger back as her face flamed red. She irritably wiped at a tear that slid down her cheek. "I stupidly let you in. Everyone always disappoints me. Why did you have to do it, too?"

Dorian was unprepared for her words—or the shame that filled him. Because she spoke the truth. He had used her. He had disappointed her.

He watched helplessly as she grabbed her purse and stalked past him. But he couldn't let her go. His hand snaked out and latched onto her arm, halting her.

She didn't fight his hold, merely stopped and looked at him. "Either tell me what I want to know or let me go."

"You ask the impossible."

"I wish you had never come into my life. I wish with everything I had that I could erase any memory of you. Because while I've been used by many, no one has hurt me like you."

She yanked her arm free. Dorian could do nothing but turn to watch her leave. With each step she took, it felt as if his world was unraveling. He didn't understand the emotions that were overwhelming him, suffocating him. All he knew was that he had to make them stop.

"You hold an object that could be the answer we need to best an enemy," he said as she walked through the door.

He held his breath as she stopped.

Turn around. Please, turn and look at me.

Air slid past his lips while relief surged through his heart when Alex pivoted toward him. She remained at the door, refusing to come back inside.

"Which one?" she demanded.

He frowned. "Enemy?"

"Artifact?"

"The one in the back corner that looks like a long oval."

Her brows snapped together. "The stone? How can that help you?"

"I doona know. It may no', but we have to try."

"We who?"

Dorian shook his head. "Why do you need to know?"

"Why do you keep it secret?"

She'd seen him, but she wouldn't say the words. He knew she was waiting on him. But he wasn't sure he could give her what she needed.

Alex swallowed and licked her lips, glancing away. "I know you can steal it any time. Why didn't you?"

"It would've been the easy thing to do, and the quickest. It's what I wanted when I first came, but then again, I have no' been out in the world in some time. The others wanted me to try and convince you to sell it."

"It was those from Dreagan who made the offer a few weeks ago, wasn't it?"

Dorian gave a single nod. "Aye."

"Why did they send you?"

She was back to the questions he didn't want to answer. But at least there was something he could share. "It was my time to rejoin my family and take my place among them."

Alex walked toward him, their gazes locked. "I'll give you the artifact. I'll hand it over right now. If only you'll tell me who you are."

She stopped before him, so close he could lean forward and claim her lips. The yearning for her went deeper than he thought possible. But it was a union that could never be.

"As you said, I could steal it any time."

It tore him up to see her struggling not to shed the tears that welled in her lovely eyes. How he could hold such disdain for humanity but care for one of them enough that he hated himself for hurting her?

"Then take it and get out of my life," she told him.

Her words cut deeper than any blade ever could. Dorian was confused and mystified at the emotions that jumbled within him. Ceana would have had the answers. His sister always had.

Alex's gaze shifted away as her tears spilled over. She took a step back and pivoted.

Dorian rushed to move around her because he couldn't stand knowing that he put the pain in her eyes and her heart.

"You saw me," he said. "The *real* me."

She refused to look at him.

"I liked when I abhorred humans. Imagine my surprise when I met one so different that I couldna hate her." Dorian swallowed as her gaze slowly lifted to his. Now that he began, he didn't want to stop—couldn't stop.

"I'm one of the first beings to inhabit this realm. I'm as old as time, an immortal dragon who has magic and the ability to shift into this form whenever I wish. I'm a Dragon King."

Chapter Fourteen

Oh, shit.

It was true. Alex blinked up at Dorian, unable to form words. In the few minutes she had been in the penthouse, she'd withstood a bevy of emotions—and she knew it was just the tip of the iceberg.

"Immortal?" she repeated.

He nodded slowly, his blond hair moving about his shoulders. "Aye."

"And you're...well, old." She winced when she heard herself, but her brain couldn't manage math at the moment.

Dorian's lips softened as he chuckled. "Aye."

"How are you so normal?"

"We sleep."

She gave him a shot of side eye. "Well, yeah. We all do."

"Nay, lass. I've been in a deep sleep for millions of years."

Her head was spinning. "I've got to sit down for this, I think."

Alex moved past him and made her way to the hunter green sofa. She sat, letting the feel of the cool leather sink through her jeans and into her.

Dorian followed cautiously, watching as if he feared she might throw herself out the window. Which, if she were honest, she might have done had she learned all of this the previous night.

Immortal. Wow. She was actually having a harder time with that than the dragon part. Because if he was immortal, that meant he would continue to live long after she died.

And while they weren't in a relationship of any kind, she might have been a bit premature and thought about what it would be like to be

Dorian's. Even that brief thought was enough to make her heart long for what she couldn't have.

Dorian moved to sit in a chair opposite her. He leaned forward, bracing his forearms on his knees. "This is why I didna want to tell you."

"It's more than that," she said, recognizing the truth. "You spoke of enemies. Enemies you didn't want me to know about."

"Aye, I did."

"The video Meg told me about, that was you?"

He drew in a quick breath and leaned back. "I only woke a week ago, but aye, that video is of the Dragon Kings."

"There is more than one of you? I don't understand. I thought there could be only one king?"

Dorian stared at her a long moment. "Are you sure you want to know this? You can no' repeat any of it. No' to Meg or Paul or anyone."

"I understand."

"No matter what they try to tell you. This stays between us."

"You have my word," she promised.

He rubbed his hands on his jean-clad thighs, his gaze dropping to the large cream-colored rug. "Everything you've been taught about your history is a lie. For eons, dragons ruled this planet." His eyes swung back to her. "Dragons of all sizes and colors. Each clan had a King."

"So you were King of your clan," she said, crossing one leg over the other.

"Aye. Each King is chosen by the magic within this realm. Only the strongest, the most powerful in each clan is chosen. Sometimes we have to issue a challenge to the current King in order to claim the throne."

Alex held up a hand. "Wait. I thought you said you were immortal."

"Only a Dragon King can kill another Dragon King. Dragons themselves are verra much mortal, though they have incredibly long life spans."

"But if you aren't a King, how can you kill another?"

There was a slight curve of his lips as he said. "Some want to be a King so badly they believe the magic has chosen them, when in fact it hasn't. Those poor souls are killed by the Dragon King."

"And the other ones? The ones who are chosen by the magic?"

"A few try to ignore their destiny, but I didna. I welcomed it. I challenged the King and won. It's a fight to the death, so someone's life is going to end."

It sounded so barbaric, but then again, it was an entire other species. Who was she to judge? "How often do new Kings take over? Every year?"

"Some Kings remain in their position for hundreds or thousands of years, while others have a shorter reign if the magic discovers one who is better able to lead."

"And what if that dragon doesn't want to be King?" she asked.

Dorian shrugged. "I've never run across one who hasna, but I imagine that they wouldna issue the challenge."

"Does the magic ever choose wrong? I mean, surely there have been some really bad Kings."

"The magic doesna just discern our power and strength. It also sees our hearts. Only those the magic deems pure enough are chosen."

Her brows shot up. "It's too bad the magic can't pick our leaders, because we seriously need to do some house cleaning. All over the world."

"I can no' disagree with you there," he said with a smile.

She stared at his mouth for a long moment, basking in the glory of his grin. "Why doesn't the magic help humans?"

"Perhaps because you are no' of this realm? It could also be that you doona have magic. I can no' answer that."

"Can you ask the magic?"

He gave a shake of his head. "The magic isna a being we converse with. It's a part of us."

That made no sense, but she would save a more in-depth discussion about that for later. "Okay. Back to the story."

"We have a King of Dragon Kings. His name is Constantine. Con is the one responsible for keeping us together."

"Where are all the dragons? I'm sorry, I'm probably moving ahead of your story, but surely if there were that many, someone would've seen one."

A great sadness came over Dorian's face. "Your kind arrived one day."

"Arrived?" she repeated, her head cocked to the side. "What do you mean?"

"One minute humans were no' there, and the next they were. The Kings were drawn to the group, and when we gathered, each of us shifted for the first time in order to communicate with your kind. Dragons speak telepathically."

She rotated her ankle. "And humans do not."

"We learned that the group held no magic, and the Kings agreed to offer protection and refuge. We realigned our territories so the mortals would have a place to live. But it soon wasna enough. They kept asking for more. Dragons became irritated and there were clashes."

Alex frowned. "I can't imagine that ended well for the humans."

"They retaliated by hunting the smallest dragons."

Her heart thudded at the anger in his voice. "Did you go after the humans then?"

"We made a vow. Once a King gives such a promise, we doona go back on it. We were able to broker a truce, but by that time, the toll had already been dealt to that clan of dragons. It wasna long before the mortals began hunting them again. By the time their King realized that he was the last, it was too late."

"And the humans couldn't kill him."

"Nay."

She didn't even know this King, but her heart broke for him. To have lost his entire clan without being able to defend them seemed wrong. "What happened to him?"

"He died when we battled each other, but I'm getting ahead of myself."

"That's...horrible."

Dorian drew in a deep breath and released it. "There were other Kings who had better experiences with mortals. Ulrik, who was like a brother to Con, had such a union. Or so we thought. Like other Kings, he took a human as his lover, and he fell in love with her. To our shock, he asked her to be his mate. Dragons mate for life, so it means something when we make such a decision."

Alex nodded, eager to hear more.

"During the early years, we learned that our seed rarely planted in the females. The few times it did, the bairns always died either in the womb, or were stillborn."

"That's awful," Alex murmured.

Dorian twisted his lips. "That was a drawback of our pairings, but what the humans didna know was that being mated to us, they became immortal. Whether we took a dragon or a human as ours, they would live until we died."

Well. She hadn't seen that bit coming. In fact, she felt a kernel of hope spring up in her heart. But Alex hastily tried to squash it. It would do no good to dream about a man, er, dragon, that she couldn't have.

"The woman Ulrik chose didna love him," Dorian continued. "She felt beholden to him for all the things he'd done for her and her family. So Ulrik's uncle, Mikkel, contrived a plan with the help of a Druid."

"Druid?" she asked before he could go on.

Dorian wrinkled his nose. "Over the course of several hundred years, a few mortals garnered magic—the Druids."

He said it as if that should answer all her questions about them. It didn't even come close. But she'd let it go for now.

"The Druid utilized a spell to be able to converse with Mikkel and they used Ulrik's woman, telling her that she needed to kill Ulrik before she was bound to him for life."

This was better than any book Alex had read in years. She uncrossed her legs and sat up straighter. "Didn't Ulrik tell her he couldn't be killed?"

"He had no reason to give her such information. But she would never get the chance. Con wasna sure her love for Ulrik was real, so he took an interest in her. He discovered her plan before she could carry it out. You need to understand that Ulrik was the best of all of us. He loved to play jokes on others, and was always laughing, always helping. Con knew the betrayal would destroy him. So Con sent him away on a mission and gathered the rest of us. As soon as we heard, we all volunteered to kill her ourselves."

Alex gaped at him. "Kill? Surely there was another option."

"After all we had done for the mortals, this was how they repaid us? Nay, Alex, there was no other way. Con said we would find the female, kill her, and that would be the end of it. Less than thirty minutes later, the deed was done."

She leaned forward, unsure of how she felt about the woman's murder. "And Ulrik? What did he say when he returned?"

"He was furious. He didna lash out at us, though."

"Of course not," she said angrily. "You're his brothers, his friends. As irate as he was, he knew you tried to help him."

Dorian scratched his jaw. "Which meant that Ulrik took his anger out on the only ones he could—the humans."

Alex slowly sat back, realization dawning. "There was a war."

"The Silvers are some of the largest dragons along with the Golds. Ulrik, as King of the Silvers, attacked immediately. Half of the Kings sided with Ulrik, while the rest of us remained with Con."

"Wait, wait," she said. "Who is the King of Golds, and why didn't he stop Ulrik?"

"It was Con. And he tried everything but fighting Ulrik himself."

She nodded in understanding. "Because if Ulrik won, he'd be King of Kings."

"Aye. Con began turning the Kings who went with Ulrik back to him. Those of us who stayed used our dragons to help defend the villages Ulrik and his Silvers attacked. It was a bloody, horrible war. Thousands of humans were slaughtered, and in turn, they went after all dragons, those defending them, and those who didna. Every time I think of the dragons who had orders to protect the mortals—who didna defend themselves when your kind attacked—I become enraged."

Alex put her hand over her mouth, her eyes pricking with tears. "Oh, God. As appalling as all that sounds, I can see it happening. Human beings can commit such horrific atrocities."

Dorian was silent for a moment, his gaze distant with his memories. "The war didna last verra long, though it felt like it. Eventually all the Kings returned to Con but Ulrik. The only way to stop Ulrik was to bind his magic and banish him from Dreagan. Con forced him to remain in human form, walking among the mortals he detested so." Dorian blinked and focused on her. "No' our finest moment. But we had other concerns. The humans intended to kill all the dragons. No' wanting to see our clans constantly fighting for their lives, we decided to send them away until things calmed down. We opened a dragon bridge so they could go to another realm."

Alex didn't take her eyes from his face. He had yet to mention his sister, and she was afraid it would be worse than anything else she'd heard thus far.

His chest expanded with his breath. "Ceana helped me gather my dragons. The young and the old were the slowest, and she stayed back with them as I led the others to the bridge. It was one of my other dragons who alerted me something was wrong. I rushed back to find a hundred humans had surrounded my sister as she protected a group of orphaned younglings who were too exhausted and scared to fly. I arrived in time to see the mortals hacking her to bits. And all the while, she protected the younglings. Just as she had protected me. She didn't fight back, didn't douse the mortals with dragon fire.

"Because she knew her sacrifice was what I needed to get the younglings to safety. I could save her. Or them."

Alex didn't even try to stop the tears as they rolled freely down her cheek. It was no wonder Dorian hated humans. And that story alone told her so much about him.

In that heartbreaking moment, she fell completely, madly, deeply in love with him.

Chapter Fifteen

It shouldn't still hurt so fiercely, so violently to talk about Ceana. But it did.

It really did.

It was as if he was still there, watching his beloved gentle sister sacrifice herself so he could get the younglings to safety.

Dorian blinked, doing his best to pull himself from the past. To his utter surprise, Alex was kneeling before him, holding his hand between hers while she cried the tears he never could—because to do so would allow the grief to take him.

And he feared he'd never come back from that.

He reached up and gently wiped away one of the tears. Dorian stared at the bit of water on his thumb, confused as to Alex's emotions.

His gaze slid back to hers. For several heartbeats he took in the sorrow, the heartache that lined every inch of her face. The same things he felt deep inside him.

"Why do you cry?" he asked, needing to know.

Alex sniffed, seemingly unfazed by his question. "Because you lost someone you loved. Because she died a horrible, needless death to save others. Because you loved her. But also because in every word that you spoke, I can see and hear the hurt you feel. And the blame you carry."

"I should've been with the younglings, no' her. I wouldna have died."

"You said your sister raised you."

Dorian nodded slowly. "Aye. She was mother and father and sister. If it hadna been for her, I wouldna be here now."

"Then don't sully her sacrifice by blaming yourself. Ceana was one of those rare individuals who thought of others before herself. She was helping you, yes, but she also saw the younglings and knew no one else was there for them."

He turned his head away and cleared his throat which was clogged with emotion. His eyes burned, his vision blurring. Then he felt something hot and wet land on his cheek.

"You were very lucky to have her," Alex said. "Between you and Ceana, the younglings survived."

He nodded as another tear fell on his face. He didn't know how long they remained locked in their positions, but when his eyes finally dried and he took a deep breath, he didn't feel the weight of shame and regret that he had carried for so long.

Dorian swiveled his head to Alex, marveling in her ability to help him with her touch, her wisdom, and her anguish for his loss.

She smiled.

He wanted to pull her against him, to press his lips against her, but he didn't. She was next to him, holding him, but he hadn't finished his story.

"Do you wish to know the rest?" he asked.

Her head nodded eagerly. "Very much."

He lowered himself on the floor next to her so they were facing each other, legs crossed and knees touching. "Once all the dragons were gone, we searched the realm for any left behind. The ones who were dead we destroyed so there was no trace of them for the humans to use."

"Did any alive get left behind?"

"Four of the largest Silver dragons who refused to cross the bridge."

She frowned as she bobbed her head. "They were that loyal to Ulrik."

"Aye. We used our magic to put them to sleep and caged them far beneath Dreagan Mountain. After, we surrounded the area of Dreagan with our magic to keep humans out and we sought our mountains."

Her eyes widened. "You each have one? There's that many of you?"

"Dreagan is comprised of sixty thousand acres, and aye, there are."

"Wow," she mouthed.

Dorian ran a hand through his hair. "The only one who remained awake was Con. He kept vigil over the land and the Silvers. After nearly a thousand years when stories of us turned to legend and myth, he went to each of us telling us we could wake if we wished. I knew I couldna do that and no' do exactly as Ulrik had done and slaughter mortals. We'd already lost the dragons, and I couldna do more damage to my brothers."

"So you didn't leave your mountain," Alex finished softly.

"The years passed. Con put a spell on us so that none of us would feel any deep emotions like love or hatred for humans."

"But it didn't work on you?"

Dorian shook his head. "My hate was already too strong."

"Another reason you remained asleep."

"Aye. I told Con the spell didna work on me, so we agreed that I would remain asleep. Through the years, we kept tabs on Ulrik, who amassed a fortune in the human world. He created a massive empire, and all the while he plotted against us. Before he left Dreagan, he promised retribution for what we'd done."

Alex rubbed the back of her knuckles over her nose. "And you let him?"

"He was Con's best friend, his brother in the truest sense of the world. Con couldna kill Ulrik when he banished him, and he couldna do it now."

"I see."

Dorian looked down at the rug they were on. "While I remained in my mountain, the other Kings battled many times. Namely to keep the humans safe in the Fae Wars."

"Fae? Really?"

He gave a nod. "Light and Dark. Their civil war destroyed their realm, so they came here. The Dark feed off the souls of mortals by literally sexing them to death."

Alex's face scrunched in revulsion. "Yuck."

"The Light only allow themselves to make love to a mortal once. While we won the Fae Wars, it helped that the Light finally sided with us. The Fae were supposed to leave here, but they didna. They took up residence in Ireland. The Dark in the lower half, the Light in the upper. The Kings watch them to keep them in check, but it's a never-ending battle. If that wasna enough, Ulrik began looking for Druids who could touch dragon magic and no' die. He finally found one who unbound his magic, which destroyed the spell Con cast."

Surprise flashed on Alex's face. "Are you telling me that the Kings began to feel things again for morals?"

"Aye. At present, nineteen have found their mates."

She laughed, the sound filling the flat. "That's good. You all deserve some happiness."

"We also discovered that Ulrik's uncle, Mikkel, remained behind. In that second that Ulrik's powers were locked, Mikkel shifted into a human."

"Is he a Dragon King now?" Alex asked.

"Nay," Dorian stated. "But he wanted it. He set out to destroy us and use Ulrik. Mikkel aligned with many humans to do his bidding, but in the end, Ulrik won with the help of his mate, a Druid with exceptionally powerful magic."

Alex leaned back against the couch and planted one foot flat on the floor, her arms wrapped around the bent leg. "Please tell me that Ulrik's banishment was lifted and he's back among you."

"He is."

"Good. I hate stories that don't have happy endings." Her smile faded as a frown furrowed her brow. "But your enemy. Is it the Dark Fae?"

He lifted one shoulder in a shrug. "They will always be an enemy. The one I speak of is actually a group. It began some months ago when an archeologist found what she thought was a dragon skeleton on Fair Isle in Scotland."

"But, wait," Alex said. "I thought you got all of them."

"We thought we did. It seems this group used magic to hold the dragon. They killed it and cloaked it from us."

Alex drew in a quick breath. "You make it sound as if they were waiting for a certain time to reveal the skeleton."

"We believe they were. Fair Isle was Dmitri's territory, so he went back to see if it was indeed a dragon. It was. Faith, the one who found the bones, and Dmitri fell in love while they dug up the skeleton. They discovered a small wooden dragon carved to look exactly like Con."

"Oh, that's not good," Alex said with a shiver.

Dorian blew out a breath. "It was the beginning of verra bad things. When a human touched the carving, their hate for us drove them to attempt to kill one of us."

"Like Ulrik's woman."

"Exactly." Dorian was impressed that Alex was keeping everything straight. "When a King touched the piece, they immediately wanted to kill mortals."

Alex hunched her shoulders up to her ears. "Like Ulrik."

"It was only with the help of a Light Fae named Rhi who encased it in magic before anyone else could touch it that things didna escalate. That's when she felt the combination of Dark and Light Fae magic as well as good and bad Druid magic."

Alex dropped her leg to the ground and sat forward. "This is your new enemy? Druids and Fae? But I don't understand. You said Ulrik is mated to a Druid."

"They've no' performed the ceremony yet, but aye, they are together. There are five more who have Druids as mates. Then there is Shara, a Dark Fae turned Light who is mated to a King."

"What about Rhi? I gather she's a friend."

Dorian ran a hand over his jaw. "Rhi was once in love with a Dragon King. He ended their relationship for reasons none of us know."

"And she continues to come around?" Alex asked, shock on her face. "Then she's still in love."

"Aye."

"But none of this makes sense. You're friends with the Druids and Light Fae. Why would they go against you?"

He stared into her hazel eyes. "It's what we're trying to find out. We think there might be a chance that this group of Druids and Fae were here during our war with the humans."

"And my artifact can help how?"

"It dates back to that time, and we think by the carvings on it that it was made by the Fae. We need to know what they've done—and just how far they intend to go with this."

Alex looked away, contemplating his words. After a few minutes her gaze returned to him. "The story you've just told me is...well, amazing. And terrifying. But I keep coming back to a couple of things I'd like answers to."

"Ask," he offered.

She shrugged and pointed to herself. "Where did we come from? To just show up? That doesn't make any kind of sense. If some kind of space ship came, wouldn't you have seen that?"

"Aye," he replied with a grin.

"And we just appeared?"

He nodded slowly. "There was no magic in any of the mortals we found, so we knew they didna use magic to get there."

"What if someone with magic sent them?"

"It's something we've considered."

Alex sighed, tapping her finger on her leg. "And the wooden dragon. To make it a replica of Con appears to mean that they're targeting him. Is it because he's King of Dragon Kings? Or something more?"

"It's likely the former, but at this point, we're imagining the worst."

"And why wait so long to come after you? It's like they wanted some kind of alignment of things to take place."

That wasn't something the Kings had thought of, at least that Dorian knew. "We have to locate the Fae involved. The Druids we know are dead since they're no' immortal, but the Fae are another matter entirely. If we can find them, we get answers."

"And the artifact I have might lead you to the Fae." She gave him a sexy smile. "Then let's go get it."

He couldn't believe what he'd just heard. "Are you sure?"

She laughed as she got to her feet and held out a hand to him. "On one condition."

"Name it."

"I go to Dreagan with you."

Chapter Sixteen

The idea had come to Alex on a whim, but now that she had put her condition out there, she really wanted to go to Scotland and see Dorian's home.

His warm brown eyes seemed to burn with more gold than usual as they stared at her. A blond brow slowly rose. "You want to see Dreagan?"

"After all you've described, yes."

There was a beat of silence. "You ran."

She took in a deep breath because she'd known he might bring this up. "I did. I was terrified. Dragons aren't supposed to be real. At least not how I've been raised. I sat all night among my artifacts thinking about you and what I'd seen. I felt an assortment of things. Fear, worry, anger, and confusion. By the time Meg arrived this morning, I was numb, unable to know what I felt, much less find a word for it. But there was one emotion that stood out."

"Anger," he replied.

Alex nodded. "I pieced together that you were there for something I had. It was Meg who pointed out that you could've hurt me at any time, but never did."

"Remind me to thank her for that."

Alex smiled at his interjection. "I know why you kept your secret. You and the other Kings have suffered enough. Whatever I have that can help is yours."

"You wouldna sell it before, but now you give it to us?"

"Now that I know what it's for, of course. I get offers for pieces in my collection all the time, and Meg knows the answer is always no without telling me about the buyers. I don't even know who makes the proposition."

Dorian flattened his lips for a heartbeat. "I have an offer. You allow me to bring the artifact, along with you, to Dreagan, but when we're finished with it, the piece returns to your collection."

"You would give it back?"

"Doona sound so surprised. Of course we would. If it can no' help us, we've no use for it."

She smiled and held out her hand. "Deal."

His long, warm fingers slid against her palm before wrapping around her hand. A moment later she was in his lap.

Her breath left in a whoosh, her free arm instinctively going around his neck. Once more against his hard chest, her body roared to life. She knew how amazing his hands were on her body, how his tongue could tease her to the point of utter bliss.

"Why shake when we can kiss?" Dorian murmured.

His eyes were on her lips. Alex's heart thumped erratically. "I couldn't agree more."

"Then stop talking," he said and pulled her head down.

As soon as their lips touched, she moaned. All the worry and distress of the night before seemed like a lifetime ago. It didn't matter that Dorian was a dragon. She knew what she felt—and the depth of the love that he had awakened.

Within moments they were breathing heavily. His fingers had pulled her hair from her bun, and she couldn't get close enough to him.

"I need inside you," he said between fiery kisses.

She nodded. "Yes."

Alex gasped when he lifted her so that she straddled him. By the time she lowered herself, both of them were naked.

"Oh."

He grinned. "I couldna wait for the time it would take to remove our clothes."

"I'm not complaining."

His arms wrapped around her, raising her. "Good."

Her hands halted their caress of his shoulders when she felt his hard cock against her. With one thrust he was inside her. She dropped her head back, her mouth opened on a silent scream of absolute pleasure.

The world around them faded away as they became lost in each other. The desire, the longing, the undeniable hunger.

Alex rotated her hips before riding him hard, his fingers digging into her. The sight of his eyes darkening with need excited her—and pushed her to give him more.

Her breasts swelled, her nipples puckering in anticipation for his touch. And he didn't disappoint. The feel of him suckling at her breast as his arousal filled her was sublime.

Ecstasy swirled low in her belly. She reached for the climax, longing to feel that powerful bliss once more.

But Dorian proved he was very much in control when he shifted them so that she knelt next to the chair, bent over the cushion. He filled her once more, pumping hard and deep twice before he stilled.

"Can you feel me, lass?" he murmured against her ear.

She nodded breathlessly.

"Say it," he demanded.

"I feel you. All of you."

His teeth slid around her lobe and gently bit down, holding for a heartbeat before letting it go with a soft suck. "I'll always be inside you."

Chills raced over her skin at his husky words that were both a promise and a warning. And she loved it.

He swiped her curls out of the way and pressed a kiss to the back of her neck. "My words excite you."

"Yes." No one else had known what she needed. She hadn't even realized it.

But somehow Dorian had.

"Then I am yours."

Her heart skipped a beat. She wanted to look into his eyes, to see if he meant what she hoped he meant. But he wouldn't let her move. Because he wasn't finished with her yet.

Anticipation mixed with eagerness when he straightened before grinding his hips against her, reminding her that he was deep inside her. As if she could forget that sensation.

One of his large hands flattened at her neck and slowly caressed downward. "Such a beautiful body. There are so many ways I want to take you."

Yes! She wanted that, needed that.

"And in every one, you will scream your pleasure."

She clenched around his arousal, trying to get him to move. In response, he reached around and pinched her nipple hard.

Alex swallowed against the searing pain that instantly turned to pleasure. "I need you."

"I can feel your wet heat."

"Please. Don't make me wait."

His chuckle was low and so seductive that it made her clit quiver. "Sometimes the best way to gain pleasure is by denying yourself what you want most until you can no' bear it another moment. And only then do you give in."

That certainly sounded like something she would like.

"You willna come until I tell you."

She closed her eyes, a smile upon her lips. "Yes."

If she thought he would begin moving, she was wrong. He remained so deep inside her that he was against her womb. To prevent her from moving her hips, he'd pressed her hard against the chair.

But she needed some friction. So she tried to move her hips. To her dismay, his hands stopped her before she could even begin.

"No moving, lass," Dorian ordered.

Being told she couldn't move only made her want to do it even more. She was so focused on remaining still that she didn't realize he'd moved his hands until his fingers slid against her labia and then up and around her aching clit.

She moaned, jerking at the contact, but his large body held her still. The delicate, constant motion of his finger back and forth on her clit had her breathing hard, her body trembling as she fought to remain unmoving.

All too quickly she felt herself tumbling toward an orgasm. She fought to keep it at bay and not give in to the wonderful pleasure she knew awaited her, but she could only last so long.

Right before the climax took her, Dorian pulled his hand away. She dragged in a ragged breath. Suddenly, he took her hands and pulled her arms back so that she raised her head.

Then he began to move. She sighed, pleased to finally feel the length of him sliding in and out of her. His tempo quickened until their bodies were rocking against each other.

With her already on the cusp of a climax, it didn't take him long to bring her right back to the brink. The sound of flesh meeting flesh, of Dorian's rough breathing only intensified the experience.

"Alex," he ground out as his thrusts became short and fast. "Now!"

The orgasm was an explosion of pure bliss, utter paradise. With every thrust, Dorian took her higher, lengthening her pleasure. He buried himself deep, wrapping an arm around her middle so that they were locked together as their bodies succumbed to the breath-stealing climax.

They remained in that position for several minutes. Dorian pulled out of her, and by the time he lifted her to hold her in his lap in the chair, they were once more clothed.

Alex rested her head on his shoulder. "I could get used to this."

"So could I."

She wanted to ask him about his declaration that he was hers. What had he meant exactly? She didn't want to assume anything. It was better for everyone involved if things were spelled out so each knew where the other stood.

But she couldn't get the words past her lips.

"I don't suppose we can stay like this forever?" she asked.

He turned his face and kissed her forehead. "Once we have the artifact at Dreagan then we can."

"You're really going to let me go with you?"

"We made a deal."

"What about Con and the others? Won't they be upset?" she asked.

He grunted and pressed his lips to her forehead again. "They'll get over it."

That made her smile. Alex sat up to look at him. "I've only been to Scotland once, and it was just to Edinburgh. I'm ready to see your land, and I know you and the others are anxious to get the artifact. Besides, the day is still young."

He stood in one fluid motion and slowly let her legs drop, though he didn't let her go. "You're a remarkable woman, Alexandra Sheridan. From the verra first, you surprised me."

"I've been called many things, but never remarkable."

"Then everyone else are fools if they doona see what I do."

At that moment, Alex thought she could walk on clouds. There was something about being with Dorian that brought the rest of the world into focus.

"I have a private plane," she said.

One side of his lips lifted in a grin. "Dreagan has helicopters, but I believe we'll need a plane. Which we should take since I can no' fly back myself."

She blinked. "You were going to fly back?"

"Aye. My gift is to turn invisible, remember."

As if being an immortal shape-shifting dragon with magic wasn't enough. "Do all the Kings have gifts?"

"Aye," he said as he set her on her feet and took her hand.

She pulled him toward the door, grabbing her purse on the way. "Tell me on the way to my place. I want to know every detail."

Chapter Seventeen

The lightness that he felt was something new and... fascinating. Dorian kept a hold of Alex. It wasn't for protection, it was for himself.

It hadn't been that long since he thought he might never see her again. Now she was back in his life. And helping him and his brothers.

He still couldn't quite believe that she would so eagerly hand over the relic. Then again, she was proving that mortals could be decent and kind.

As they reached the lobby, he held her back and looked out of the lift. His gaze landed on Meg, who put away her mobile phone and stood when she saw them. Paul and Tim stood on either side of the double glass doors. Dorian glanced at Alex, who stared at him with clear hazel eyes.

His grin widened when he took in her hair. Her hands reached up and she began laughing loudly, covering her mouth with one hand while her eyes bulged.

"Make them wait," she said between fits of laughter.

When Dorian's gaze slid back to the lobby, Meg and Tim were smiling while Paul sulked. That didn't even annoy Dorian. He was in an exceptional mood. All because one beautiful, beguiling human had shoved aside her fear and had given him a chance.

"Okay," Alex said.

His head swung to her to find her still grinning but her hair back in place. He held out his hand, which she took, and they walked into the lobby together.

"Shall I clear your schedule again today?" Meg asked as Alex neared.

Alex glanced at him. "Actually, you might want to clear it for the foreseeable future. We're taking a trip to Scotland."

Dorian watched the assistant carefully. Meg's dark eyes jerked to him, though she still wore a smile. Meg also knew his secret, but for some inexplicable reason he trusted her.

"Good," Meg said to him before she returned her gaze to Alex. "When do you leave?"

"Within the hour," Dorian said.

Paul stepped forward. "We're going to need longer than that."

"I'll be going to Dorian's estate," Alex told the bodyguard. "That means you and the others can finally have a vacation."

Dorian waited until he caught Paul's blue eyes. "There's nowhere safer than Dreagan for her. You have my word."

"He's right," Meg said as she turned to Paul.

Alex's smile was a little tight as she looked at everyone. "Then it's settled."

"Don't you need to pack?" Paul asked Dorian.

"Paul," Alex admonished.

Dorian gave her a shake of his head. Then he walked to the bodyguard. "I have everything I need, but I appreciate your concern."

There was a moment of tense silence before Paul gave a slight nod of his head. Tim opened the doors and walked out first. Meg was next with Alex behind her and Dorian following. Paul brought up the rear.

Dorian's eyes immediately scanned the street for any threat that might come for Alex. He was so focused on others that he didn't notice the danger that was among them.

It was Meg's startled scream as she dove to the side that caught Dorian's attention. He turned to find Tim lying face down on the ground with a pool of blood widening beneath him.

By pure reaction alone Dorian grabbed Alex and spun her around toward Paul, who had already pulled his gun. Dorian pushed Alex into the bodyguard's arms and turned around, ready to put an end to these attacks.

When he found himself staring into the angry face of Alex's longtime driver, Yasser, Dorian frowned in confusion. But the resentment sparking in the driver's gaze changed everything.

Dorian laughed at the mortal. "This will be the last time you'll ever be close enough to do Alex any harm."

"I'm not after Alex," Yasser said right before his arm came down and a blade pierced Dorian.

He knocked Yassar away, delight filling Dorian when the puny mortal fell to the ground. The human rose up on one elbow and raised his gaze to Dorian.

"It's time for the Dragon Kings to fall."

Yasser's words halted Dorian. He didn't know how the driver knew who he was, but that mattered not. A little visit from another Dragon King could wipe the human's memories.

A subtle stinging began that grew rapidly. Dorian looked at the offensive blade and jerked it out of his chest. Right before he tossed it aside, he looked at the handle. The Fae markings gave him pause. Dorian's eyes jerked back to Yasser.

The driver began laughing. Dorian blinked as everything became fuzzy. He swayed, trying to stay on his feet, but his legs gave out. His knees hit the pavement so hard that he felt his kneecaps shatter.

He didn't feel the pain. Even the stinging had stopped. And that terrified him. Something was happening—and that something was magic.

Right as Dorian pitched forward, he heard Alex scream his name.

* * * *

Alex yanked out of Paul's arms and rushed to Dorian. She turned him over as the sound of sirens filled the air. There was so much blood.

"Dorian? Dorian, please. I need you to wake up. Look at me," she urged frantically.

There were people all around her, some shouting, some talking, but she heard none of it. She kept her hand over the wound, trying to staunch the flow of blood.

"Dorian, please," she begged through the blur of tears.

Someone grabbed her. Without thinking, she twisted and punched whoever it was and returned to Dorian. He was supposed to be immortal. Nothing killed him but another Dragon King.

That's what he'd said. She hadn't dreamed it. Maybe he just needed to die and then he'd wake. Yes. That was it. He'd wake. He was immortal.

"Alex?"

She ignored the voice, waiting for Dorian's eyes to pop open and for him to laugh off what happened.

"Alex."

"What?" she snapped and turned to find Paul along with a policeman holding a rag to his bloodied nose.

Paul swallowed, worry in his gaze. "They need to get to Dorian."

She followed his finger to the paramedics who stood waiting. This couldn't be happening. Dorian was a dragon. No, he was a Dragon King.

Alex couldn't help him, but maybe someone else could. She tried to get to her feet. It was Paul who helped her up and moved her out of the way. She stood numbly, watching the paramedics attempt to stop the bleeding.

Yasser was in handcuffs. He had killed Delroy and Leon, as well as Tim. Meg only had a scrape on her arm from the blade since she had ducked when she realized what was happening.

"Dorian's going to be fine," Paul assured her.

She wrapped her arms around herself. It wasn't time for her to stand idly by waiting for others to take control. She needed to do it.

Alex turned to the officer that she'd hit. "My apologies for striking you. If you wish to charge me, I understand. My assistant," she said, motioning to Meg who was being seen to in the back of an ambulance, "will give you the name of my lawyer."

"You weren't being malicious, Miss Sheridan," the officer said. "No charges will be filed."

She swallowed and wiped at the tears. "Thank you. I'll double my donation to the NYPD this year." She turned to look at Yasser, who sat in the back of a patrol car. "Whatever you need from me or anyone who works with me to help make sure that maniac never breathes free air, let me know."

"Yes, ma'am," he said.

Alex then walked to Meg, her gaze locking on Dorian. "How are you?"

"It's a scratch," she replied. "And Dorian?"

Alex shrugged and realized that Paul stood beside her. She looked at Meg before she rushed back to Dorian's side. "I need the number to Dreagan."

Meg shot her a quick smile. "Already placed the call while they were tending to me."

"You're worth your weight in gold."

Meg reached out and took Alex's hand. "Go to him. I've called the hospital. He'll be put in a special wing away from others."

"Thank you."

Paul put his hand on her back. "They're loading him. We need to go now."

"I'll be there as soon as I can," Meg hollered.

Alex lifted a hand to let her friend know she heard her as she and Paul ran to the ambulance. Then she was inside, sitting next to an unconscious Dorian in the vehicle as the sirens blared and it sped down the streets.

She couldn't take her eyes from Dorian. He was pale, so very pale. Something must be wrong, because he shouldn't be lying there like he was dying.

Like he was mortal.

She tuned out the medics as they spoke in a special code. But even she understood that things weren't good for Dorian.

An eternity later, after winding through traffic and taking back roads, they finally arrived at the hospital. She and Paul were the first out the back of the ambulance. They moved to the side, waiting for the staff to take Dorian into the emergency room.

Once he was rolled out, they followed Dorian inside only to be brought to a halt by a tall man with piercing gray eyes and light brown hair styled to perfection. She knew immediately he was a Dragon King.

"I'm Mr. Dreagan's personal physician," the man told the hospital staff in a thick Scottish brogue. "I travel everywhere with him. Thanks to Miss Sheridan, I was alerted of his accident."

Alex stepped forward and looked at the ID the man presented to her. She frowned up at him and whispered. "How do you pronounce that?"

One side of his lips lifted in a grin. "Kinnay."

She looked at the spelling, wondering how in the world Cináed was Kinnay, but she would figure that out later. Louder, she said, "I was also assured that Dorian would have privacy."

"Already taken care of," an older woman with short graying hair said as she walked up. "This way, please."

Staff took hold of the gurney and began to roll Dorian away. The other Dragon King motioned Alex and Paul to follow.

Inside the elevator, everyone was silent. Alex saw the concern on Cináed's face as he stared at Dorian. Once the doors opened and they stepped out, the quiet assaulted Alex after the noise and pandemonium of below.

In short order, Dorian was put in a room where several people dressed in operating gear waited. The woman who'd led them up here and the Dragon King spoke quietly. A moment later, the woman and the orderlies left.

Now alone, Cináed walked to Alex. "I'm one of Dorian's friends."

"I figured. Can you help him?" she asked. Then shook her head. "Sorry. I'm Alex Sheridan."

He gave her a small smile filled with understanding. "That's what we're trying to determine."

"And they are?" she asked, pointing to the nurses.

Suddenly, all but one of the group inside the room disappeared. A woman of incredible beauty with long black hair and green-gold eyes stood there. Her shoulders drooped. She lifted a hand to wipe at her hair, and Alex spotted finger rings.

Cináed moved in front of Alex to get her attention. "I'm hoping that by knowing to call us that you are aware of who Dorian is."

"A Dragon King," she replied.

"Good," Cináed said with a sigh. "I wasna looking forward to explaining all of that." He ran a hand down his face. "I need to know details. Ryder is pulling camera footage, but I want to know from both of you."

Alex nodded, wanting to help any way she could. She then glanced behind her to see Paul. She'd completely forgotten that he was there. "Is Dorian going to be all right?"

"I doona know," Cináed replied. "It would help if we had the weapon."

She gaped, feeling stupid for not even thinking about that. "Oh, God. I don't even know where it is."

"I swiped it," Paul said as he stepped around her and pulled something from his suit jacket.

Cináed smiled. "Nice work."

The Dragon King walked away, leaving Alex and Paul alone. With even fewer answers than before.

Chapter Eighteen

"Now do you think you can tell me what's going on?"

Alex swiveled her head to Paul and met his gaze. "What do you mean?"

"I thought you trusted me," Paul said, disappointment lining his face.

She glanced at the room where Dorian lay alone. "I do, but it isn't my story to tell."

Paul swiped a hand down his face before he put his hands on his hips. "I heard Yasser, Alex. I heard him tell Dorian that it was time Dragon Kings fell. Is that some gang? A mob name? Give me something."

"We're no' a crime family nor have any affiliation with one," said an authoritative voice.

Alex and Paul turned as one toward the man. His impassive black eyes stared at them as he stood in an olive colored suit with a white dress shirt beneath and no tie. He lifted his hand from his pocket and Alex spotted a gold cufflink, but she couldn't make out what it was.

Upon closer inspection she saw the gold dragon head. The man tilted his head of wavy blond locks as he lifted a brow to Alex.

She swallowed nervously as the man moved a few steps closer. He barely paid Paul any notice. Alex was used to being inspected, but she was comprehending that she stood before another Dragon King, who was determining if she was worthy or not. She really hoped she was.

"I don't know how this happened," she hurried to say, feeling guiltier as the minutes passed.

The man's brow furrowed. "This isna on you, Miss Sheridan."

"Alex, please," she told him.

He held out his hand. "I'm Constantine."

In her life, Alex had met presidents, queens and other royalty, and numerous heads of states, and not a single one of them had ever made her nervous. Until now.

Con bowed his head slightly, the only acknowledgement that she must have let it show that she knew who he was. His hand remained outstretched, and she quickly took it.

She then looked into his dark eyes and said, "We were on the way to my place to get some things before we headed to Dreagan."

It wasn't that Alex didn't trust Paul... Well, that wasn't entirely true. Right now, she only trusted the Kings after her driver of six years turned out to be a murderer. So she kept any mention of the artifact from Paul, but Con was smart enough to get what she had purposefully left out.

"Shall I send someone to gather what you need?" he asked.

Before Alex could reply, Paul said, "No one is going into her home but me. Not after what happened."

Con's shift was subtle, but Alex saw the way he stiffened and his lips went into a firm line as he turned to Paul.

It wasn't long before Paul looked away, unable to hold Con's gaze. Then again, Con was the King of Dragon Kings. Paul didn't stand a chance against any of them.

"I would appreciate that," she told Con, bringing his attention back to her. "However, I would like for you to take my assistant with you. Meg knows exactly what is needed."

The tall woman from earlier walked toward them. She smiled easily at Alex. "I wish we could've met under better circumstances. I'm Eilish. It's a pleasure, Alexandra."

"Call me Alex," she replied, hearing the slight Irish brogue mixed with the very American accent.

"She's Irish, but was raised in Boston," a man said as he came to stand between Con and Eilish. "I'm Ulrik, by the way."

Alex's mouth dropped open as she stared. Ulrik's gold eyes crinkled as he looked at Eilish. "I fear she knows all about me, love."

"You are rather a troublemaker," Eilish replied.

Alex snapped her mouth closed. "I'm sorry. I'm being incredibly rude."

A moment later the elevator opened and Meg walked out. Alex introduced both Meg and Paul to the others all while glancing toward

Dorian.

"We'll figure out what happened," Ulrik said.

She looked toward him and saw the promise in his eyes. "It was Yasser, my driver. He's been with me for a while. I trusted him. I don't understand what happened."

Meg touched her arm. "It's going to be all right. I'm going to head to the penthouse now."

Alex watched her friend leave with Ulrik and Eilish. When she turned back around she discovered that Cináed had taken Paul off to talk about the weapon. Which left her alone with Con.

"Do I make you nervous?" he asked.

She wrapped her arms around herself, her gaze going to Dorian. "A little. I just found out who Dorian was. I told him that I was handing the relic over to see if it could help all of you. No one knew who he was but me and Meg."

"And how did the two of you know?"

Alex swallowed and walked into the room to be with Dorian. She stopped by his bed and took one of his hands in hers. Then she looked at Con, who stood on the opposite side. "I saw him shift. Then he disappeared. I got scared and left. It was Meg who told me about the video that circulated recently. She also helped me see that Dorian had the opportunity to hurt me, but he hadn't. That's when I realized he'd come for something. My anger overruled everything else and I went to see him."

She smoothed a lock of hair from Dorian's brow. "He told me everything, including how his sister was killed. My heart broke for him." Her gaze slid to Con. "For all of you, actually."

"I saw for myself how he looked at you from the recordings of the accident."

She nodded. "I understand his hate. To have that much loathing within him, and not harm anyone in this city is amazing. New York tends to bring out the worst in most people. You took a huge chance."

"I had faith in him."

"You took a chance."

Con blew out a breath and nodded once. "I took a chance. We needed the artifact, and Dorian was the only one who could get through the security and magic to it. He wanted to steal it his first night here. He actually walked your penthouse and found the relic."

"Magic?" she asked, confused. "There's no magic around it."

"Aye, there is."

She licked her lips. "I don't know how it got there. Yasser knew who Dorian was. I need to know how."

"We're looking into that."

"There was such hate in Yasser's eyes. He'd been nice to Dorian until that moment. I never suspected."

Con shrugged at her words. "You hire others to protect you."

"Yes, but I pay a firm a large amount of cash to vet those who work for me. Ultimately, this falls on me."

"Nay," the King of Kings said. "It's mine. No' only did I send Dorian out into the world when he wasna ready, but I knew our enemies were out there, waiting."

Alex twisted her lips. "The thing is, Dorian was ready. He didn't know it then, but he needed this. As for enemies, that will never change. I have my own share, and no matter what I do, they're always there. What I need to know is if Dorian will wake up. He's immortal. He's not supposed to die."

Cináed walked in the room then. He looked between her and Con. "I thought this might be like the wooden dragon Dmitri and Faith found, but it isna. There are Fae markings on the hilt."

Con briefly closed his eyes and whispered, "Rhi."

Alex frowned, wondering what was going on. She recognized the name from the story Dorian had told her, but she couldn't remember exactly who Rhi was. Everyone seemed to be waiting expectantly, but nothing happened.

The minutes ticked by in silence. Alex looked between the two men. She was about to ask what where Paul was when Con opened his eyes, anger flashing briefly. Cináed appeared resigned.

"I should've known," Con mumbled.

"Should've known what?" came a feminine Irish voice behind Alex.

She whirled around and came face to face with a creature so stunning that Alex blinked, thinking she was in a dream.

The woman's silver eyes landed briefly on Alex before she tugged on the long black braid that hung over one shoulder.

She smiled at Alex, but as her silver eyes moved past her, the grin died. The woman frowned and came to stand beside Alex to look at Dorian.

"Thanks for coming, Rhi," Cináed said. "We wanted you to look at this."

Rhi didn't look to him. Instead, she lifted her gaze to Con. "You woke Dorian?"

"I had no choice."

She snorted. "There's always a choice. What did you need that you made him come to this city?"

"I didna make him do anything," Con said, his voice low, his body still as stone.

Alex sensed the anger rolling off him, but she kept silent, watching and listening.

Con and Rhi stared at each other a long moment. Then Rhi said, "So this is what you've been doing? Instead of us going after UBitch, you're doing"—Rhi waved her arms—"what exactly?"

"Getting an artifact from me that dates back to the wooden dragon," Alex said.

Rhi's head swung to her. Her gaze lowered to see Alex's hold on Dorian's hand. Silver eyes jerked back up to Alex, narrowing slightly. "And you are?"

"Alexandra Sheridan," she replied.

Rhi returned her attention to Con. "Where's the artifact?"

"That's no' why Con called for you," Cináed said. "This is."

Rhi physically jerked back a step at the sight of the black knife. "Get that away from me."

"Why?" Con demanded. "What is it?"

Rhi's face contorted with revulsion and even fear as she shook her head, taking another step back.

Alex tightened her hand on Dorian. "Tell him," she beseeched Rhi. "Dorian was stabbed with that."

"For fek's sake," Rhi murmured and turned her head away. After a moment, she took a deep breath and faced them. "That," she said, pointing to the weapon, "is a Fae blade."

A muscle twitched in Con's jaw. "We gathered that bit."

Rhi cut her eyes to him. "I've only ever seen pictures of it. The handle used to be white and gold with a large diamond at the tip."

Cináed lifted it with two fingers. "It's all black now."

"It was the weapon used by the first Fae murderer. All the evil of his deed went into that weapon and turned it black, like his heart."

Alex contemplated the weapon as Rhi spoke. "Sort of like our Cain and Abel?"

"Yes," Rhi replied. She shivered. "We need to get that weapon somewhere it can't influence any of us. As far as I knew, the blade was lost in history."

Alex stared in amazement as Con took the weapon and enveloped it a glowing, transparent box. Cináed took the box and strode out of the room.

"Who stabbed Dorian?" Rhi asked.

Alex swallowed loudly. "My driver. He said it was time the Dragon Kings fell after he thrust the blade into him."

"Where is the wound?" Rhi demanded.

Con lowered the sheet that covered Dorian and tore open the bloodied shirt. The blood had stopped, but now the wound was turning black. And spreading.

Rhi moved closer for a better look. Then she asked Con, "Have you tried to heal him?"

"You can do that?" Alex asked, shock and anger making her forget who she was talking to. "That's your gift, and you let him lie here like this? How dare you?"

Rhi's smile was blinding. "Oh, honey, I like you."

Con held Alex's gaze for a heartbeat before he put his hand on Dorian and closed his eyes.

Chapter Nineteen

Dorian dove from the sky breathing dragon fire on the approaching Dark Fae. Their screams of pain were music to his ears. He dipped a wing and swung back around before he landed.

Orbs of dark magic slammed into him, burning like acid through his scales and into his muscle and bone. But there wasn't time to think of the pain when more and more Dark Fae came.

He swung his tail, cutting a dozen of his enemies in half. With every one he killed, ten more took their place. They kept coming, like ants, never stopping, never hesitating.

Dorian didn't know how long he battled, didn't consider how deep his pain went before he realized something was wrong.

Other Dragon Kings should be with him. They would never leave him alone to battle so many. He opened the mental link and called for help. But there was no answer.

Only a laugh that chilled him to the bone.

It was a sound filled with delight. And triumph.

It was also distinctly female.

He hated the sound of it. Why couldn't he have heard Alex's laugh?

At the thought of her, his mind exploded with his memories of her—right up until the blade plunged in his chest and he'd fallen.

This battle wasn't real, but it didn't make the agony of the Dark's magic any less when it hit him. He tried to ignore the Dark Fae, but that was a mistake.

They swarmed him, climbing onto him and bombarding him with their orbs. He roared and jumped into the sky, tucking his wings and rolling through the air to dislodge them. A lucky few managed to hang on.

He quickly rid himself of them by flying so close to the mountains that he scraped his own scales. Fortunately, the Fae couldn't hang on after coming in contact with the rocks.

Dorian then flew straight up, getting lost in the clouds until he could no longer see the ground below him. He had no idea where he was, but he knew how to get home. He headed in the direction of Dreagan.

No matter what, a dragon always felt the pulse of magic that resonated up from Dreagan. Dorian didn't pause, didn't rest. He flew hard and fast toward his home, thinking of Alex and his brethren.

Something was seriously amiss. He didn't know how he'd left New York and Alex, but he had. Something or some*one* had seen to that.

The laugh sounded again. He growled, instantly wanting to stop it.

When he found who was responsible, he was going to douse them in dragon fire. It didn't matter if they were mortal or some other being. They. Would. Die.

As soon as he reached Dreagan, he began his descent from the clouds. The smell of smoke and burning flesh reached him first.

He was so shocked by the smell that was so reminiscent of the war with the humans that he actually drew up short, flying in place as he let himself come to grips with what was happening.

His wounds from the Dark Fae had healed, but the revolting stinging remained. If there were more Fae waiting for him, he needed to be prepared. In the next heartbeat, Dorian used his power and turned invisible.

Only then did he leave the clouds. The smoke was so thick over Dreagan that even his dragon eyesight couldn't penetrate it. Finally, he emerged from it. And his heart clutched painfully in his chest when he saw that Dreagan was gone.

The manor was a demolished, burning ruin while smoke billowed not only from the scorched Dragonwood but from every mountain, as if someone had gone inside each of the Kings' sanctuaries and destroyed them. He could hardly comprehend what he saw. No one should have been able to do this to Dreagan.

The anger that built inside him at the destruction came to a screeching halt when he saw his dead brethren scattered over the land.

He roared his anguish and grief. Dorian landed hard, the ache of disbelief slamming into him. He wanted to scream, to cry. To hit something.

Instead, he slammed his hands upon the earth, threw back his head and roared. But that did nothing to ease his misery.

Slowly, he walked among his brothers. He paused when he came to Ulrik. Still in dragon form, Ulrik had fallen, but it looked as if he were reaching for something. Dorian followed Ulrik's outstretched hand and spotted Eilish.

Dorian frowned and raised his head. He'd been so focused on the Dragon Kings that he hadn't noticed the dead mates lying among them.

While he didn't know what had killed the Kings, the mates had died first. Each had their upper torso caved in. Almost like something was thrown at them.

Eilish and Ulrik weren't mated yet, so Dorian understood why the Druid could have been killed. But as he stood over Cassie and Elena, who had the same wounds, it didn't make sense.

They had undergone the mating ceremony and had the dragon eye tattoo on their upper left arms to prove it. That mark gave them immortality. So how had they died?

Who had killed the Dragon Kings?

And who had destroyed Dreagan?

Through the smoke that drifted over the land he saw someone walking toward him. Dorian didn't shift into his human form. Whoever it was would deal with him in his true shape.

To his surprise, it was a woman. As she drew closer he recognized that she was Fae. He took in her long black hair and the comely shape of her face.

There was much to appreciate about a Fae—Dark or Light. They were gorgeous. Even the males. There wasn't an ugly one among them, but that didn't mean their souls weren't hideous.

Dorian raked his gaze over the female's body. She wore a long black coat that billowed around her, showing off the tight, black dress that hugged her body and the tan suede boots that came over her knees.

She walked as if she had all the time in the world. As if the death and devastation around them meant nothing. That's when he knew she was responsible.

"It's about time you came," she said in her Irish accent as she drew near.

He didn't even try talking to her. It wasn't as if she could understand him.

"Oh, I understand you fine, Dorian." She smiled slowly, her silver eyes locked with his.

"Who are you?" he demanded.

She shrugged. "You might know had you not withdrawn yourself from the others. They needed you."

"I'm here. I answered Con's call."

"Not the first time." She shrugged, her face scrunching. "Or the second. You chose to ignore him. Your King."

He stalked forward until he towered over her. *"Who are you?!"*

She looked up at him and smiled. "Rhi."

"I know your name. You are friend to the Kings."

"Afraid you have that wrong, big guy. I *used* to be friend to the Kings. Then, I let the darkness have me. I kill planets now."

Dorian couldn't believe what he was hearing. He shook his head. *"Why?"*

Her smile was gone, replaced with that of utter evil. "Unrequited love has a shelf life, handsome."

"Is this where you kill me?"

She threw back her head and laughed. It was the same sound he'd heard earlier, the same laugh that sickened him. Then her silver gaze landed on him and he saw her begin to glow.

Dorian drew in a breath and blew out dragon fire. If he was going to die, he wasn't going down without a fight.

There was a bright flash and he bellowed as arms grabbed him. He fought with all his might, hitting and kicking.

"Dorian!"

He paused, realizing only then that he was in human form. It took several tries before his eyes focused and he found himself in a small room with Con and Ulrik holding him pinned to the wall.

His eyes scanned the room, jerking back to the door when he spotted blond curls peeking around Cináed's arm. "Alex?"

"I'm here," she said and ducked past Cináed before he could grab her.

Dorian grinned when she yanked on Con and Ulrik until they released him. As soon as Alex's arms went around him, Dorian closed his eyes and held her close.

"What happened?" he asked.

"Some bad juju, handsome."

His eyes snapped open at the Irish accent. The tall woman strolled into the room and leaned against the wall next to Cináed.

"You're lucky," the Fae said.

Dorian shoved Alex behind him and faced the female. "Who are you?"

"Oh, sorry," she said with a wince. "I forget we've never met. I'm Rhi."

He shook his head as he let out a loud grunt. "Nay, you are no'."

She gave him a scathing look. "Ah, yeah, I am. I've been me for, well, *ever*. I think I'd know."

"She is Rhi," Con said. "Why did you say she isna?"

Dorian rubbed his forehead. What was real and what wasn't? He wasn't sure anymore. Was this the dream and the other place real?

Alex came to stand before him once more. "You gotta tell us what's going on. You've been out for hours. We didn't think you'd wake."

"What changed?" he asked, gazing deep into her hazel eyes. She grounded him, her touch clearing his head of all the horrible things he'd witnessed.

"The artifact," Ulrik told him. "Con tried to heal you, but his magic did nothing. We brought the relic in here to discuss it and what to do with you. That's when we noticed that whenever we brought it near you that it drew out the evil."

That got his attention. "Evil?"

"The blade that struck you was from the first Fae murder," Rhi said. "It's been missing for ages."

"Or someone was saving it," Con said.

Dorian squeezed his eyes closed for a moment. "I was in a place that seemed verra real."

"What place?" Alex asked.

He glanced at her before looking around the room. "Earth, but drastically different. I fought waves of Dark Fae. They were everywhere. I got away and flew to Dreagan. Only when I got there it was destroyed. Every mate had been viciously murdered."

"Doona stop," Ulrik said when Dorian paused.

Dorian wasn't sure he could get out the next part. Alex linked her fingers with his and gave him a nod. Dorian pressed his lips together as the image of his brothers lying dead flashed in his mind.

"All of you were dead," he said.

Merrill raked a hand through his hair. "Fuck me."

"Tell us everything. Every detail," Con said.

Dorian slid his gaze to Rhi. "A woman appeared. I knew she was Fae instantly. She said her name was Rhi. She claimed responsibility for all the death and claimed to kill realms. Right before I woke, she began to glow."

Ulrik strode to Rhi and pointed at her. "Is this the face you saw, Dorian?"

"Excuse me," Rhi said in outrage and shoved Ulrik's hand away. She walked closer to Dorian and looked at him. "Was it me you saw?"

He shook his head. "Nay."

"Did the Fae say why she killed everyone?" Con asked.

Dorian tightened his grip on Alex. "She said that unrequited love had a shelf life."

"You've got to be shitting me," Rhi ground out angrily. She held out her hand as a mobile appeared. After typing something she held up the small screen to Dorian. "Is this the crazy bitch you spoke with?"

As soon as he saw the face, he recognized her. "Aye. That's the woman."

Rhi blew out a breath and looked at Con. "UBitch strikes again."

"Who is UBitch?" Alex asked.

Ulrik sighed loudly. "Rhi means Usaeil."

"Queen of the Light?" Dorian asked in shock.

There was death in Con's eyes when he said, "The verra one."

Chapter Twenty

"Where is Yasser?" Dorian demanded.

Alex was still reeling from listening to Dorian speak of what he'd seen in his dream. Or was it a dream? Had it been a vision of the future? A ploy of some sort? She honestly didn't know.

She glanced up from the floor to see that everyone was staring at her. Alex raised her brows. "What?"

"Where is Dorian's would-be killer?" Con asked.

She shrugged helplessly. "At one of the police departments."

"I need to speak with him."

Alex looked at Dorian. "You say that as if you think you'll get past the guards to talk to him. And let's not forget that Yasser has the right to refuse you. Only attorneys get in to see potential clients."

The smile on Dorian's face was anything but nice. "It's a good thing we know a verra good lawyer then."

Somehow she wasn't at all surprised at the news. "Is he also a Dragon King?"

"Of course," Ulrik said.

"Of course," she mimicked beneath her breath.

New York society couldn't compare to the ego or confidence of the Dragon Kings. The simple fact was that no one could compare to them.

And they knew it.

They could take over the world, but they didn't. They chose to hide, to protect their identities and their way of life at all costs.

When Alex looked at Dorian, he was grinning at her. She elbowed him and tried not to smile, but he pulled her close and rested his head against hers.

Out of the corner of her eye she saw the others watching with varying expressions of surprise, delight, and sadness. It was Rhi's despondency that bothered Alex the most. Despite only meeting the Light Fae, Alex liked her warrior spirit and her grace, not to mention Rhi's style. Alex would never be able to pull off the all-black ensemble that both Rhi and Eilish carried to perfection.

"I'll get Vaughn," Ulrik said and touched something on his wrist before disappearing.

Alex jerked back. "Can all of you do that?"

"No, they can't," Rhi quickly said. "Only Ulrik because he has a bracelet given to him by a Fae that allows him to do it. Eilish can because of her finger rings. But teleporting is something all Fae can do."

While she spoke, Alex saw Con's lips lift in what could have been considered a cunning grin, as if he had a secret others didn't know. Since he was the King of Kings, Alex imagined he had a boatload of secrets.

"I still don't see how you're going to get in to talk to Yasser," Alex told Dorian. "Vaughn might be able to talk to him, but that's all."

Dorian turned her so he could look into her eyes. "Do you so easily forget what I can do?"

To remind her, he released his hold on her and vanished. A hand grasped hers and he gradually came back into focus.

"I can go anywhere, do anything without anyone seeing me," he explained. "My magic bends matter. In this form or my real one. What I can no' do is touch anything or I'll be seen."

"Is that why you didn't steal the artifact?"

He shook his head. "I didna steal it because I didna want to do that to you."

"Ugh. Just kiss already," Rhi said and turned on her heel to walk to the wall.

Cináed shot Rhi a dark look before he told Alex and Dorian, "Ignore her. And keep talking."

Alex felt her face heat as she blushed. "Perhaps we save this for later."

"Why?" Dorian asked. "I couldna care who sees me kiss you."

She didn't stop him when he placed his lips on hers.

"Talk about timing," Ulrik said with a laugh.

Alex turned her head to find Ulrik standing with yet another Dragon King.

"Vaughn," Dorian said in greeting.

Alex took in the King wearing a gray suit with a white shirt and a solid purple tie with matching pocket square. Vaughn's light brown hair was trimmed short on the sides but the top was longer, showing the thick tresses that were carefully styled.

Eyes a brilliant Persian blue locked on her. "It's a pleasure to meet you, Alex. I'm Vaughn."

She smiled at him in greeting. Then looked at Dorian. "I know you have to do this, but I want to be there. He worked for me. He duped me all these years."

When Dorian didn't reply, Alex hastily continued. "You'll be there. Both you and Vaughn. What can Yasser do?"

"A lot actually," Vaughn interjected. "However, I think he'll want to talk to you. I was going to suggest you come."

Alex shot him a surprised look, focusing back on Dorian. "Well, there goes my argument. However, if Yasser knows of the Dragon Kings, then he'll realize Vaughn is one as well."

"Both Vaughn and Alex are right," Con said.

Rhi nodded, her nose wrinkled. "Of course Alex is right. And just for good measure, I'll be tagging along."

"We doona need everyone there," Con said in a low voice tinged with just a slight edge of aggravation.

Rhi shrugged. "Try and stop me."

"I'd like Rhi there," Dorian said. "It was a Fae blade he had, and one thing we need to learn is where he got it."

"We're going to be great friends," Rhi said as she shot Dorian a wink.

Alex turned to the others. "It's settled then. Shall we go?"

"No' like that," Vaughn said, pointedly looking at her clothes.

She glanced down and found blood on her and her hands. How could she have forgotten about that? She held out her arms, looking around for a sink when Rhi walked up and clasped her hands.

"Look at me," Rhi urged with a soft smile.

Alex did as she was bade.

Rhi's smile grew. "You know, I've been to a party or two with you. Your style is something to be envied. I saw the men looking at you with yearning and the women staring with envy. And you were oblivious to it all. You always stood apart. Why?"

"It's better that way," Alex replied.

Rhi made a face and sighed loudly. "Well, I hate to be the one to break it to you, heiress, but you'll never stand alone now."

With that, Rhi dropped her arms and backed up. Alex glanced down and found herself not only clean, but in a black pantsuit with a white sheer shirt beneath and a black pair of Christian Louboutin spiked heels.

Rhi winked at her when Alex looked up. "I had to add in a bit of myself."

Alex didn't know what to say. She turned her head to Dorian and felt her hair down. Reaching up, she realized that not only had her hair been done, but she had on different jewelry as well.

"This is amazing. Thank you," she told Rhi.

The Fae beamed. "I had entirely too much fun doing it. But, let me say before Con cuts me off, we need to go shopping together."

"Deal," Alex replied with a smile.

Rhi then looked around the room, her gaze falling on Con last. "I'll be with the mortal waiting on the others."

And then she was gone. Alex wished she had that ability. How easy it would be to travel. Just a thought, and she could be wherever she wanted.

"Ready?" Ulrik asked as he, Vaughn, and Dorian waited for her.

Alex didn't have time to answer as they linked hands with Ulrik taking one of hers and Dorian the other. When she blinked, they were in another location. She gazed up at the tall brick building before hastily looking around.

"What if someone saw us?" she asked worriedly.

Ulrik flattened his lips. "It's New York. No one notices anything."

He did have a point. Still, Alex looked around, waiting for one of the police walking past to yell that they had just appeared, but nothing happened.

"Let's go," Vaughn said as he strode around the side of the building.

Dorian gave her a nod. "I'll be behind you the entire time."

Alex swallowed and glanced at Ulrik before she followed Vaughn into the police station. When asked for her identification, her heart skipped a beat because she didn't have her purse. She had no idea where it was.

But without missing a beat, Vaughn slid both of their credentials to the officer. In a matter of minutes they were led through a serious of locked doors before they found themselves in a room.

Vaughn motioned for her to sit while he stood in the corner. "As you said, he'll probably talk to you first. Let's see how he reacts by no' knowing I'm here."

She drew in a breath and pulled out the chair to sit at the table. Alex hated how nervous she was. She knew Yasser couldn't hurt her in here, but she didn't want to be around him, didn't want to talk to him.

But right now wasn't about her. It was about the Dragon Kings and what Yasser had tried to do to Dorian.

Alex squared her shoulders when she heard the lock on the door open.

"You're no' alone," Dorian whispered in her ear. "I'm here, Alex. I'll always be next to you."

How she wanted to touch him, but she didn't dare reach for him. Her head swung to the door as it opened. Yasser was led inside by a uniformed officer.

The cuffs and chains that bound her former driver were fitting, and she prayed that they remained on him for the rest of his miserable life.

Yasser smiled when he saw her. "I knew you'd come."

She didn't say anything as he was led to the chair and cuffs locked his bound hands to a bar on the table. The officers remained, and that simply wouldn't do.

If she was going to do this properly, then she needed to come at Yasser as if it was a regular business negotiation and leave all personal feelings behind.

And it was likely going to be one of the most difficult things she'd ever done.

Alex looked at each of them. "Thank you, gentlemen. If you would be so kind as to leave us, I would appreciate it."

She didn't worry about anyone listening or any recording devices. Dorian and the others would take care of that.

Once the officers left, Alex focused on the murderer. "Who are you really?"

"I fooled you," he said with a laugh. "Not once did you even think I was anything other than what I said I was."

Alex folded her hands in her lap. "Yes, you did fool me. Bravo. Why?"

"There's been one of us in your family's employ ever since the Immortal Stone fell into your family's hands."

Alex tried not to let her surprise show, but she wasn't sure she was successful. Knowing the real name was also a boon. "Because?"

Yasser laughed. "We knew that eventually the Kings would seek it out. All we had to do was wait."

"You keep saying we. So there are more of you?"

Yasser narrowed his gaze as he slouched in the chair. "There are, and before you ask how many, I won't tell you."

"Because you don't know." It had been a guess, but by the tightening of his lips, she knew she'd been right. "Do you want the artifact?"

He snorted loudly, looking away. "We made sure it went to your family. That was the only way the Kings would ever find it." His gaze slid back to her, a sinister smile on his face. "Tell me, Alex, how is Dorian faring?"

She didn't take the bait, though it was difficult. "Why do you hate the Dragon Kings so?"

"You really have to ask that?" Yasser gave an irritated shake of his head. "No one should have that kind of power. We got rid of most of the dragons. It's just a matter of time before the Kings fall. We've already begun our assault."

Chapter Twenty-one

Dorian seethed with rage as he stood behind Alex glaring at Yasser. How he wanted to rip the mortal's head off.

"What's the next step for your group?" Alex asked.

Dorian couldn't believe how calm she was. He was impressed at her composure and how no matter how Yasser tried, he couldn't ruffle her.

"As if I'd tell you."

With his fists clenched, Dorian fought not to slam the murderer's head against the table. It would ease the anger inside him but do nothing in getting them answers.

Alex exhaled and leaned forward to rest her arms on the table. "It feels good to best them, doesn't it?"

"That's not going to work," Yasser said.

Alex frowned and gave him a confused look. "What do you mean?"

"Trying to make me believe you don't like the Kings. I saw the way you looked at Dorian. It didn't take him any time to get you out of your clothes and riding him."

"That's rather crude," Alex stated icily.

Dorian quite agreed. He glanced at Vaughn to find his friend watching Yasser intently. Yasser had locked his gaze on Alex the moment he entered the room and hadn't looked away. Dorian didn't know if the man realized Vaughn was there or not.

No one was better at being a solicitor than Vaughn. He handled every nuance of the law—international, as he did now, as well as domestic—and he did all it brilliantly with class and style that couldn't be duplicated.

And many had tried.

"You seem to know an awful lot," Alex said, bringing Dorian's attention back to her.

Yasser sneered at her. "You didn't hide anything from those who worked for you. You were an open book. It was almost too damn easy."

"Hmm," Alex said, lifting her eyes to the ceiling briefly. "Perhaps I should point out that you're also an open book. Your narrow-mindedness is pathetic."

Yasser lunged forward, jerking against the chains that held him. "And you're tainted now that you've had one of *them* between your legs."

At his move, Dorian took a step toward him. Hell, even Vaughn pushed away from the wall. But Alex didn't so much as twitch. She'd known her words would get a reaction.

Damn, she was good, Dorian thought. He smiled proudly at his woman. Because she was his. He just needed to let her know.

"You're upset because you're the one who wanted in my bed," Alex stated.

Dorian's gaze swung to Yasser, who was bent over the table glaring at Alex. His nostrils flared, but he didn't deny her words.

Alex slowly sat back and crossed one leg over the other, never taking her eyes off him. "As you know, Yasser, money can do a great many things. Every year I give a very large donation to the NYPD. Then there are the lawyers. I know the district attorney personally, and I can be sure to give him every little bit of evidence he needs to nail your ass to the wall."

"Trying to scare me?" the ex-driver asked with a bark of laughter. He hooked his foot around the leg of the chair and brought it toward him. He sat and shook his head. "It's not going to work."

"I'm not finished," Alex said, her tone becoming hard and unforgiving. "You murdered three people, and attempted to murder another. You will be convicted. All the evidence they need is in witness statements and on the many cameras around the area."

"That's already been taken care of," Yasser said with a smile.

Dorian jerked his head to the side and said, "*Vaughn.*"

"*Already talking to Ryder,*" Vaughn replied via their link. "*The wanker is right. Someone was trying to take care of it. Ryder beat them to it, however.*"

Quietly Dorian moved to stand beside Alex. He bent and whispered, "No' going to happen."

Alex flashed Yasser a bright smile. "Good luck with that."

"You think they won't erase the footage?" the murderer asked.

"I think you've overestimated your group, but really you've underestimated the Dragon Kings."

Yasser shrugged, uncaring what she had to say.

Alex regarded him a long, quiet moment. "Let me get back to what I was telling you. You *will* go to prison. When you do, I can make certain that your life is a living hell. You can't imagine the various atrocities committed daily in prison. You will suffer each and every one for the rest of your life."

Dorian was shocked at Alex's words, but he shouldn't have been. His woman was a fierce one, and the world was just getting a taste of what he'd seen of her.

"Or," Alex said. "You tell us where you got the weapon and where to find your people, and I'll make sure you're left alone."

Yasser shook his head. "No."

Dorian was tired of standing on the sidelines and watching. He was a fucking Dragon King. He should be *doing* something.

"*Wait,*" Vaughn said in his head, as if he knew what Dorian was about to do.

"*Why?*"

"*I have a feeling Rhi is about to make an appearance. No' to mention Alex is getting us much more than I ever could. She's good, Dorian. Verra good.*"

Dorian's chest puffed out with pride. "*I know.*"

"*So let her keep doing it.*"

As much as it rankled Dorian, Vaughn was right. There was a time and a place, and right now wasn't the time for the Kings. "*I'll save this for when we find these wankers.*"

Vaughn slid his gaze toward where he thought Dorian was and smiled.

It was good to be back with his brothers. Dorian wished he hadn't waited so long, but he was with them now and in the fight as he was supposed to be. These evil Druids and Fae weren't going to know what hit them when the Kings finally located them.

It was just a matter of time.

Then Dorian remembered what he'd seen with Usaeil and the dead Kings. Had that been a glimpse of the future? Of a possibility that *could* happen if the Kings didn't set something right?

He didn't know, and it was driving him mad. Because he had a feeling what he saw was a possible outcome for the Kings. And it scared the hell out of him.

Alex tilted her head to the side. "When I walk out of here, the offer I'm giving expires. If you don't help me, from the second my feet cross that threshold, you're going to believe you're in Hell."

"Your threats don't scare me," Yasser said with a derisive sneer.

Rhi suddenly appeared sitting on the table next to the mortal. "Mine should."

Yasser fell sideways out of his chair, his mouth opening and closing in fear.

Rhi pushed herself off the table and came to stand over him, putting the heel of her stiletto shoe on his balls and pressing slightly. "I can hurt you this way, mortal. Or I can hurt you with magic."

He vigorously shook his head and tried to roll to the side to cover his privates.

But Rhi was having none of it. "Shall I show you my magic?"

"No, no," Yasser hurried to say. "I know you're Fae."

Rhi exchanged a look with Alex and Vaughn before smiling at the human. "Do you now?"

"Yes," he said eagerly. "I know all about the Fae. We follow you."

What the shite? Dorian moved closer to Alex. He wanted to touch her, but he kept his hands to himself. It was the fact she was in the same room with a man who had used her and her entire family that worried him.

"Tell me everything," Rhi demanded.

And to Dorian's surprise, the mortal agreed.

Yasser sat up and looked at Alex. "Why didn't you tell me you were working with the Fae? I would've told you everything."

"You thought you knew me," Alex said as she got to her feet. "You knew nothing."

"I'm waiting," Rhi said before Yasser could reply to Alex. "Tell me about the weapon."

Yasser frowned. "I don't understand."

"What's there to get?" Rhi asked. "I posed a question, and now you answer it."

"But," Yasser said looking between Rhi and Alex. "You're the one who gave it to me."

The room went as quiet as death. Dorian only knew Rhi by name.

He'd been asleep during her and her lover's affair—and the ending of it. But he knew how many times she had helped the Kings through the years.

Yet, it was the second time something pointed to Rhi being the culprit in all of this.

"When?" Rhi demanded of Yasser. "When did I give you the weapon?"

The mortal swallowed loudly. "Two nights ago you came to me and said the time was now. You put it in my hands. Why can't you remember?"

"I do," Rhi said, lifting her chin and taking her foot from him. "I just wanted to make sure you knew the facts."

"Oh, I do," Yasser assured her.

Alex looked nervously at Rhi and then over her shoulder at Vaughn. Dorian wanted to get everyone out. Something had gone seriously wrong, and they needed to figure out what that was before they continued this discussion with the ex-driver.

"I'm still waiting for you to tell me about your group," Alex said.

Yasser looked at Rhi, who gave him a nod.

Dorian held his breath, waiting for the human to give them what they wanted.

"We're Druids," he began. "We've always been aligned with the Fae."

"Go on," Alex urged when he paused.

Yasser's eyes bugged out as he opened his mouth and began choking. Black goo came spilling out of his mouth and onto the table.

Without regard to who might be watching or listening, Dorian grabbed Alex as Vaughn joined him.

"Rhi," Dorian shouted.

The Fae was with them in the next heartbeat, and then they were at Dreagan in Con's office. Dorian looked down at Alex, whose face crumpled as she threw her arms around him.

"You were amazing," he whispered as he rubbed his hands up and down her back. "Simply amazing."

"She was bloody brilliant," Vaughn said.

Dorian looked at Rhi, who stood beside them, her gaze a million miles away. He moved Alex away when it looked as if Rhi was glowing.

No one said anything until Con, Cináed, and Ulrik strode in. The three paused at the sight of Rhi. It was Con who moved to stand in front of her.

She lifted her gaze to him. "It wasn't me."

"Someone tell me what happened?" Con asked without looking away from Rhi.

Vaughn squeezed the bridge of his nose with his thumb and forefinger. "Yasser recognized Rhi when she showed herself. Alex was doing a good job of getting Yasser to talk, but he wouldn't tell her anything because of her association with Dorian."

"So Rhi stepped in," Dorian continued. "As soon as he saw her, his fear was palpable. Rhi asked about the blade, and he said she's the one who gave it to him."

"It wasn't me," Rhi said again. "I've never seen that mortal before."

Alex moved around Dorian and came to stand beside Rhi. Hesitantly, Alex put a hand on the Fae, much as Rhi had done her earlier. "You're glowing."

Rhi's gaze swung to Alex, and instantly the glowing ceased. "I swear, I wasn't part of it."

"We know," Con said.

Ulrik blew out a long breath. "And we know just who is responsible."

"Usaeil," Dorian said.

Chapter Twenty-two

Why did everything keep coming back to the Light Queen? Alex studied Rhi, who somehow held it all together, but she was a kettle that was about to blow.

"Why is Usaeil doing this?" Alex asked.

Cináed's face creased with disgust. "Because she's a liar who wants everything."

"Because she's a power-hungry bitch," Ulrik added.

Rhi turned her head to Alex. "The truth is that she wants Con, and won't be satisfied until he's hers."

"So she's going after you?" Alex asked, looking from Rhi to Dorian. "That doesn't make sense."

Con walked to his desk and pulled out the chair before lowering himself into the seat. He leaned back, crossing an ankle over his knee. "You're only getting a portion of the story, Alex. There are a lot of sides to Usaeil. I seemed to have lost my mind for a wee bit and took her as my lover with the understanding that it was just a fling."

"She didna get the message," Dorian interjected.

Ulrik issued a bark of laughter. "That's putting it mildly."

Alex slid her gaze back to Con, waiting for him to continue. There was much more she didn't know, but she was insanely curious to figure it all out.

Con waited until the others were finished. Then he said, "Usaeil is on a mission to have us mated. She believes the Fae are the ones who can give us children."

"Oh," Alex murmured.

Dorian had spoken of that, but she hadn't thought much about children since they had made love. She'd been too wrapped up in the man—dragon—himself.

"Usaeil is focused on me because she thinks Con and I are sleeping together," Rhi said. "We're not, but Ubitch just can't seem to get that through her head."

Alex nodded, understanding dawning. "So Usaeil is jealous of you."

"Exactly," Dorian stated.

Alex crossed her arms over her chest. "Rhi, the picture you showed Dorian in New York was of an actress. A very famous, very *American* actress."

The eyeroll Rhi gave was epic. "I'm afraid to disappoint you, but that's very much Usaeil. She wants and needs to be adored by millions. What better way to do that than to become an actress? Fae have the ability to use glamour to change our appearance."

"Which is what Usaeil did when she gave Yasser the weapon," Alex said. "Wow. She's quite the piece of work."

"She used me," Dorian said.

Con quirked a brow. "Join the club. All Usaeil does is use people to her own ends. I fell into the trap without even realizing it. Now, everyone at Dreagan is paying the price."

"Many others as well," Rhi added.

Alex reached for Dorian's hand. "Do we know if she's always been involved with this group that Yasser was a part of?"

"I wish I could say no, but I can't," Rhi said. "Usaeil isn't the queen I thought she was."

Con shook his head. "Usaeil hasna been the queen you needed for a verra long time."

"If ever," Ulrik added.

Alex leaned against Dorian when he pulled her against him. It felt good to have him near as the whirlwind of this new world spun around her. He was the rock that she clung to, the unfaltering one who would always steady her.

"With Yasser dead, we still doona have any answers," Dorian said into the silence of the room.

Cináed grinned. "No' totally back to square one. We have a distinct advantage—Ryder."

"Get him on Yasser's trail for as far back as Ryder can go," Con ordered. "That's where we'll find Yasser's connection to this group."

Cináed gave a nod and left.

Ulrik looked from Con to Rhi. "Things are heating up."

"I'm ready to go after Usaeil now," Rhi said.

Con shook his head. "No' yet. We're learning more of her involvement. We need to know why."

"That can be found out after we have her," Dorian added.

Alex's gaze moved from one to the other as they spoke. Rhi was obviously more than ready and willing to take her revenge on the queen, but Con hesitated. Alex didn't believe it was out of fear, but more of caution.

Con had everyone at Dreagan to think about while Rhi was only concerned with herself. Alex didn't understand why the two were working together, but it must have something to do with Usaeil.

"I'm going to get Eilish and see if we can find out anything on the Druids in New York," Ulrik said.

Rhi sighed. "And I'm going to start cleaning up this mess so no one thinks Alex is a murderer."

Before Alex could reply, Rhi disappeared. Alex was aware that it was just she and Dorian with Con now. She cleared her throat. "I need to call Meg. She's going to need to know where to bring the artifact, or Immortal Stone as Yasser called it."

"She's already here," Con said. "Eilish brought her, along with the relic, after the hospital."

"Good." Alex shifted feet.

The last time she had been so uncomfortable and nervous was when she'd stood before her father for a punishment.

Con rose to his feet and came to stand before her. "Thank you for helping us, but more importantly, I want to give my appreciation for all that you did for Dorian when he was attacked."

Her heart warmed when Dorian's arm tightened around her. She smiled up at Con. "I did what most people would do."

"Perhaps," Con said with a slight twist of his lips. "We will be indebted to you forever."

Alex shook her head. "That's not necessary. As I told Dorian, the artifact is yours for however long you need it. It was just sitting in a case with me. Here, it could be put to some good. So use it. And while I believe your estate far exceeds mine monetarily, I do have vast connections. Let me know if I can help. That way Dreagan remains on the sidelines and the focus is on me."

A genuine smile turned up Con's lips. "Thank you. Truly. We will take you up on that offer if something should arise." Con's gaze shifted to Dorian. "Welcome back, brother."

Alex stared after Con's retreating back. She turned to face Dorian. "I had no idea when the day began that I'd learn your secret, watch my employees murdered, think you had died, see you come to life, meet a Druid and a Fae, not to mention Con and the other Dragon Kings, interrogate a murderer, learn of the Queen of the Fae, and watch my driver die by some mysterious magic. And while I did expect to be at Dreagan, I had no idea I would be teleported here."

"Are you tired?" he asked with a grin.

She thought about that a moment before shaking her head. "Oddly no. I'm wired."

"Adrenaline. When that dies down, you'll crash."

"I know. Until then, I want to see where you live."

He waved an arm around. "This is Con's office."

"No," she said with a laugh. "I want to see your mountain."

Dorian's face lined with confusion. "Why would you want to see that?"

"I want to know everything about you."

"How about I show you my chambers here? There's a nice bed," he said with a seductive grin.

She caressed her hands up his chest and around his shoulders. "Since when do we need a bed?"

"Ach, woman. Doona talk like that or I'll take you right here."

Alex rose up on her toes, smiling before she gave him a quick kiss. "Are you needed?"

"They'll let me know if I am."

"Well, then?" she asked.

Dorian captured her lips in a searing kiss that ended entirely too soon. "Come," he said as he took her hand.

Alex was led out of the office into a wide corridor. Everywhere her eyes landed there were dragons—some plainly visible while others were hidden. From paintings to tapestries to sconces, dragons played a huge part of Dreagan.

She was so focused on finding all the dragons that she paid little attention to the rest of the manor as Dorian led her through a maze of halls, stairs, and doorways until they were outside.

Her mouth dropped open as she stared at the grandeur of Dreagan in the vibrant red and orange sky of the sunset. Mountains surrounded them, most still with peaks covered in snow. A large wood extended to her left, silently urging her to walk among the old trees and explore.

"Tomorrow, I'll show you everything in the day," Dorian said as he looked at her. "But I wanted you to see it immediately."

She was completely awed. "I have no words to describe the wild beauty before me."

His smile widened. "Are you ready?"

"Ready?" she asked with a frown. "For what?"

No sooner had her words left her mouth than something flew over her, whipping her hair around her face. She clawed at the strands so she could see.

"Oh, my God," she murmured when her gaze took in the six dragons flying above them, all in different colors. Her head swiveled to Dorian. "Will you join them?"

"Later. My preferred time is at night. While some love the sun on their scales, I want the moon."

She faced him, sliding her arms around his waist. "You are truly one of a kind. I'm one lucky girl to have you walk into my life."

"Nay, lass. I'm the lucky one. You mended both my mind and my heart. I was on a destructive path. Con knew it and tried to help me, but I refused to listen to him or anyone else. But one afternoon with you, and everything changed."

She smiled brightly. "It was the gelato, but I'll happily take the credit."

"I'm sorry I used you."

Alex smoothed the frown lines from his forehead. "You had good reason. If our positions were reversed, I'd probably do the same. Others were only after things to forward their own self-interests."

"I'm trying to apologize. You should let me," he said, his lips flattening in a firm line.

She lifted a shoulder. "I'd rather you kiss me."

Dorian lowered his head. Just before their lips met, she said, "And maybe show me that bed you spoke of."

He groaned low in his chest and yanked her against him, his lips slanting over her mouth. The kiss was filled with desire, with hope, and with love.

She didn't care that the dragons flying around them could see. All that mattered was the Dragon King in her arms.

And the love that continued to grow in her heart.

Alex wanted to tell him of her feelings, but she didn't want the kisses to stop.

"Need you," Dorian said gruffly. "Now."

"Yes."

In the next second, she found herself flying. Wind stung her wet lips as she looked up at Dorian in all his dragon glory as he gently held her in his large claw while they flew over the land.

Alex shifted to see between the slit in his digits as they passed the jagged mountains and rolling glens. Excitement kicked up when he descended toward a peak. She tried to keep her eyes open when he dove through a hole at the top of the mountain.

She gaped in glee when his wings spread, bringing them to a halt. He landed gently and set her down. As soon as her feet hit the ground, she found herself staring at a naked Dorian.

"Oh, yes," she murmured as she kicked off her shoes and rushed into his arms.

Chapter Twenty-three

The ease in which he could breathe and think was astounding. Dorian hadn't realized how much hate had weighed him down—or ruled him.

A fire crackled, its red-orange glow covering Alex's body. He smiled and held her tighter against him while watching the shadows cast by the flames on the wall.

Alex's finger drew lazy circles on his chest. Neither had spoken after they had made love. He hoped she would be the one to bring up their future, but she had remained quiet. Much to his chagrin.

All the eons he had spent in his mountain made him forget basic things—like telling a woman that he'd fallen deeply, madly in love with her. It had hit him with the force of an exploding star, but felt as comforting and right as the moonlight upon his scales.

"I didna woo you."

Her hand paused, then she lifted her head to look at him. "I beg your pardon?"

Dorian looked into her hazel eyes and sighed. "I didna woo you. No' as I should have. I was too wrapped up in my revulsion of humans, too filled with hatred to realize what I needed."

"You were filled with grief. There's a difference."

He rolled her onto her back and leaned over her. "There's no'. Aye, I still grieve for my sister, but it was hate that I fed."

Alex raised a hand and set it on his jaw before slowly lowering her arm. "And now?"

"I'm learning to put aside my loathing."

"It's a start," she replied with a smile.

Dorian swallowed, anxiety tying his stomach in knots. "When do you have to return to New York?"

She blinked up at him several times. "There's no timetable."

One obstacle overcome. Now, if only he could get the words out. It shouldn't be so hard to tell someone you cared about how you felt. He knew she was fond of him, but no words of love had been exchanged.

"I...," he began and paused. "I'm no' a man with pretty words. I doona know how to give you poetry or even know when to say things correctly. What I'm trying to tell you, badly, is that I'm in love with you, lass."

The slow smile that spread over her face made his heart leap with hope. "I think you say exactly the right thing every time. You may not give me flowery words, but you've let me know in many ways that you cared for me. It was in your words, in your gaze, and even the way you held me. Just like when you said you'd always stand with me. I knew then that you felt something."

"But you never said anything."

Alex pushed at his shoulder and flipped him on his back before straddling him. "I did. It was in everything I said and everything I did. Yet I had every intention of telling you that I love you, that I can't imagine life without you, and I don't care how long I have with you as long as we're together."

Dorian sat up and cupped her face. "I should've seen your love as you saw mine."

"I'll tell you every day. And I'll show you as well."

His heart swelled with so much love that he thought it might burst. "And I you, lass."

He pulled her head down and kissed her slowly, thoroughly. His cock hardened, yearning to be inside her once more.

But before he claimed her body again, he had more he wanted to say.

Dorian tore his mouth from hers and waited until her eyes opened. "I doona want to face another day without you. I want you as my mate, lass. I want to be bound to you. I know without a doubt you were meant to be mine."

She began to answer, but he put a finger over her lips. "Understand that we mate for life. There's no going back once the ceremony has been completed. You need to be certain."

Alex tugged his hand away. "There is one thing I've never been more sure about, Dorian, and that's you. I know I've still got a lot to learn about your life and the Dragon Kings, but this is where I want to be. I feel it in my soul that I'm meant to be here with you. And I can help. I want to help. I want to be with you. Only you."

"I can no' wait to find out what our life together will be."

She laughed huskily. "Oh, babe. We've already begun. Didn't you know that?"

"We'll argue."

Alex shrugged and nipped at his lips. "Of course we will. But think of the make-up sex."

"Mmm," he said kissing her neck.

"I'll want to stand with you on everything. You can't stop me. I'm used to being my own woman and answering to no one but myself."

Dorian leaned back and grinned. "Love, if I fear for you, I'll try to stop you. It's just how I'm made. But as I told you, I'll always stand with you. No matter who or what we face, be it mortals or immortals. We do it together."

"Together," she whispered.

He moaned as she ran her tongue over his lips. Dorian knew that life would never be the same again. But it was going to be glorious and full of love.

Epilogue

The next day...

"Was it a dream?" Dorian demanded. "Was my interaction with Usaeil just a fantasy?"

Rhi drew in a breath, irritation clear on her face. "For the third fekking time, I don't know."

Dorian slapped his hand against his thigh before he paced Con's office. Alex sat in the chair next to Rhi while Con stood quietly staring out the office windows.

The question had plagued Dorian since he woke from the stabbing. It relentlessly troubled him, waking him in the middle of sleep or coming out of the blue while he was discussing something else entirely.

He stopped and leaned back against the wall. "None of you saw it. Everything here that we know and love wasna just gone, but annihilated. Like a child demolishing a toy. The Dragonwood was burned to nothing, and smoke was everywhere. Even our caverns within our mountains had been gutted."

Con slowly turned to him.

Dorian glanced at Alex. She'd heard all of this before. She was the one who'd urged him to talk to Con and Rhi. Alex thought Rhi might be able to help him distinguish between a vision and a dream.

He cleared his throat against the rise of emotion. "The mates were savagely murdered, and the Dragon Kings were lying dead near them."

"Did you see Con?" Rhi asked.

Dorian frowned as he shook his head. "I stood next to Ulrik and

Eilish. I saw so many dead."

"But you didn't see Con," Rhi said as she pushed up from the chair and approached him.

"I doona think so."

Con asked Rhi, "Why does that matter?"

"Because I think this was a trick by Usaeil." Rhi shrugged, her lips twisting. "It's a guess, actually. I don't want you to get your hopes up, Dorian, because it could have very well been a vision of what might happen. But it also sounds like something Usaeil would do. She wants Con, so she won't hurt him."

"But she does want to hurt you," Alex pointed out to Rhi. Her hazel gaze turned to Dorian. "Did you see Rhi?"

He shook his head again. "I don't recall noticing her. Actually, I didna see the mates until after I found the Kings."

"No Rhi and no me," Con said as he crossed his arms over his chest. "That could mean anything if this was a trick by Usaeil. It could mean that she wanted Rhi to die another way."

"Or expected me to be dead by another hand," Rhi said.

Alex jumped up and came to stand beside Dorian. "I'm confused now. What?"

But Dorian understood. He turned Alex to face him. "We all know, but can no' prove yet, that Usaeil gave Yasser the weapon. The queen could have added the spell that would show whoever was stabbed exactly what was shown to me. It's why you were no' in there. Or Rhi. Because she believes Rhi will die another way."

"Oh," Alex said with a nod. "That makes sense."

Rhi puffed out her cheeks before releasing the breath. "But it doesn't tell us how she got the damn weapon to begin with."

"I'm just hoping it's no' a premonition of what's to come," Dorian said.

Con dropped his arms. "Always be prepared for any eventuality. It's the only way we're going to survive this."

Alex's gaze came to rest on him before she asked, "Feel better about this now?"

"Aye," Dorian replied.

"Good, because I'm dying to see what we can learn about the artifact and if it will help."

Damn. He'd been so focused on his dream that he'd momentarily forgotten the Immortality Stone. Without wasting another moment, he grabbed her hand and gave a nod to Con.

It wasn't long before the four of them stood in a cavern in Dreagan Mountain where the artifact was being held while encased in layers of dragon magic.

"Was this wise?" Rhi asked.

Dorian frowned. "Nothing is stronger than dragon magic."

The Light Fae snorted and slid her gaze to Con.

The King of Dragon Kings pulled his hand from his pocket, holding something round and gold within his palm. "We know there is magic surrounding it. It didna hurt either Eilish or Ulrik, but I wasna going to take any chances after the wooden dragon."

"Or the dagger," Rhi added.

Dorian gave a nod to the relic. "What can you tell us, Rhi?"

"Nothing as long as there is dragon magic surrounding it. I've got to be able to touch it if I'm going to tell you what kind of magic is involved." She swung her head to Con. "Unless Eilish or Ulrik already know that."

There was a beat of silence before Con removed the dragon magic around the Immortality Stone. Dorian positioned himself a little in front of Alex in case he needed to shield her from anything.

Rhi moved toward the waist-high boulder that the artifact rested on and walked slowly around it, her eyes taking in details of the relic. Finally, she paused and put her hand over it.

After a heartbeat, she lowered her hand and stepped back. Worry lined her face while concern filled her silver eyes.

"Is it that bad?" Alex asked.

Rhi sighed as she shook her head. "It is Fae writing. And while I can sense the magic surrounding it, I can't feel what kind it is."

"Neither could Ulrik," Dorian said.

"I wonder," Alex murmured as she took a step toward it.

Dorian stopped her, not wanting her to get close.

She smiled at him. "It's been in my family for generations. Not once has it hurt any of us. I've handled it multiple times."

Dorian reluctantly released her, but Alex didn't move from his side. Instead, she intertwined her fingers with his. The action made him breathe easier.

Alex then said, "A Druid and a Dragon King attempted to touch it while it was under my security. A Fae just tried to see about the magic now."

"Your point," Con said.

But Dorian understood now. "Each one of us has gone separately. What happens if a King and a Fae look into the magic together?"

"Oh," Rhi said with her brows raised. "Good idea, Alex."

While his woman beamed, Dorian began to move toward the stone. But it was Con who stepped up beside Rhi.

"You should let me," Dorian told him.

The King of Kings shook his head. "If anyone is going to get hurt, it's me."

"Oh, let's not worry about me," Rhi said with a grumble.

Con shot her a dark look before they both put a hand over the artifact. Rhi sucked in a breath while Con frowned.

"Well?" Dorian urged. He hated not knowing what was going on.

Rhi licked her lips. "The magic is...."

"Intense," Con finished for her.

The Fae nodded. "It's not Fae or Druid or dragon."

"But I sense aspects of all three," Con added.

"More dragon than anything."

"Aye."

Dorian was more confused than ever. "What does this mean? That a dragon is now part of the group?"

Con lowered his hand and met Dorian's gaze. "This magic is the same as we feel on Dreagan. It has facets of Druid and Fae magic because they're on this realm with us."

"Are you saying this isn't bad magic like the wooden dragon?" Alex asked.

Rhi rested her hand on the artifact and smiled. "That's exactly what he's saying. Besides, it saved Dorian's life."

"If it's no' meant to harm us, why was it kept from us?" Dorian wanted to know.

"To lure you to me," Alex replied.

Con took the stone from Rhi. "Can you read the writing?" he asked.

"Some," she replied. "I need more time."

"You'll have it." Con turned to Dorian. "The Immortality Stone needs to be kept safe."

Alex lifted her chin. "Without a doubt. It also belongs on Dreagan. Consider the artifact now the property of the Dragon Kings."

There was more discussion on how to read the writing, but Dorian wasn't really listening. He couldn't take his eyes off his woman. And he couldn't wait until they were bound to each other.

"I like when you smile," Alex whispered.

"You give me a reason."

She rose up and gave him a quick kiss. "I want to put Meg in charge of everything in New York so I can remain here."

"Is that something Meg wants?"

Alex grinned and nodded. "She's anxious to return so she can take over her new role."

"You doona have to do that. You can return anytime you want."

She glanced at Con and Rhi still deep in conversation before she pulled Dorian from the cavern. "All my life I've wanted a quiet place in the country to live. You've not only given me love, Dorian, but you gave me a dream you didn't know I had. I'm sure I'll return to New York every once in a while, but I don't need to go back. I've got everything I need right here."

He wrapped his arms around her and yanked her against him. "I love you, Alexandra Sheridan."

"And I you."

His lips found hers as they kissed, giving in to not only the passion, but the love that bound them tighter than anything else ever could.

* * * *

Also from 1001 Dark Nights and Donna Grant, discover Dragon King, Dragon Fever, and Dragon Burn.

Sign up for the 1001 Dark Nights Newsletter
and be entered to win a Tiffany Key necklace.

There's a contest every month!

Go to www.1001DarkNights.com for more information.

As a bonus, all subscribers will receive a free copy of
Discovery Bundle Three
Featuring stories by
Sidney Bristol, Darcy Burke, T. Gephart
Stacey Kennedy, Adriana Locke
JB Salsbury, and Erika Wilde

Discover 1001 Dark Nights Collection Five

Go to www.1001DarkNights.com for more information.

BLAZE ERUPTING by Rebecca Zanetti
Scorpius Syndrome/A Brigade Novella

ROUGH RIDE by Kristen Ashley
A Chaos Novella

HAWKYN by Larissa Ione
A Demonica Underworld Novella

RIDE DIRTY by Laura Kaye
A Raven Riders Novella

ROME'S CHANCE by Joanna Wylde
A Reapers MC Novella

THE MARRIAGE ARRANGEMENT by Jennifer Probst
A Marriage to a Billionaire Novella

SURRENDER by Elisabeth Naughton
A House of Sin Novella

INKED NIGHT by Carrie Ann Ryan
A Montgomery Ink Novella

ENVY by Rachel Van Dyken
An Eagle Elite Novella

PROTECTED by Lexi Blake
A Masters and Mercenaries Novella

THE PRINCE by Jennifer L. Armentrout
A Wicked Novella

PLEASE ME by J. Kenner
A Stark Ever After Novella

WOUND TIGHT by Lorelei James
A Rough Riders/Blacktop Cowboys Novella®

STRONG by Kylie Scott
A Stage Dive Novella

DRAGON NIGHT by Donna Grant
A Dark Kings Novella

TEMPTING BROOKE by Kristen Proby
A Big Sky Novella

HAUNTED BE THE HOLIDAYS by Heather Graham
A Krewe of Hunters Novella

CONTROL by K. Bromberg
An Everyday Heroes Novella

HUNKY HEARTBREAKER by Kendall Ryan
A Whiskey Kisses Novella

THE DARKEST CAPTIVE by Gena Showalter
A Lords of the Underworld Novella

Discover 1001 Dark Nights Collection One

Go to www.1001DarkNights.com for more information.

FOREVER WICKED by Shayla Black
CRIMSON TWILIGHT by Heather Graham
CAPTURED IN SURRENDER by Liliana Hart
SILENT BITE: A SCANGUARDS WEDDING by Tina Folsom
DUNGEON GAMES by Lexi Blake
AZAGOTH by Larissa Ione
NEED YOU NOW by Lisa Renee Jones
SHOW ME, BABY by Cherise Sinclair
ROPED IN by Lorelei James
TEMPTED BY MIDNIGHT by Lara Adrian
THE FLAME by Christopher Rice
CARESS OF DARKNESS by Julie Kenner

Also from 1001 Dark Nights

TAME ME by J. Kenner

Discover 1001 Dark Nights Collection Two

Go to www.1001DarkNights.com for more information.

WICKED WOLF by Carrie Ann Ryan
WHEN IRISH EYES ARE HAUNTING by Heather Graham
EASY WITH YOU by Kristen Proby
MASTER OF FREEDOM by Cherise Sinclair
CARESS OF PLEASURE by Julie Kenner
ADORED by Lexi Blake
HADES by Larissa Ione
RAVAGED by Elisabeth Naughton
DREAM OF YOU by Jennifer L. Armentrout
STRIPPED DOWN by Lorelei James
RAGE/KILLIAN by Alexandra Ivy/Laura Wright
DRAGON KING by Donna Grant
PURE WICKED by Shayla Black
HARD AS STEEL by Laura Kaye
STROKE OF MIDNIGHT by Lara Adrian
ALL HALLOWS EVE by Heather Graham
KISS THE FLAME by Christopher Rice
DARING HER LOVE by Melissa Foster
TEASED by Rebecca Zanetti
THE PROMISE OF SURRENDER by Liliana Hart

Also from 1001 Dark Nights

THE SURRENDER GATE By Christopher Rice
SERVICING THE TARGET By Cherise Sinclair

Discover 1001 Dark Nights Collection Three

Go to www.1001DarkNights.com for more information.

HIDDEN INK by Carrie Ann Ryan
BLOOD ON THE BAYOU by Heather Graham
SEARCHING FOR MINE by Jennifer Probst
DANCE OF DESIRE by Christopher Rice
ROUGH RHYTHM by Tessa Bailey
DEVOTED by Lexi Blake
Z by Larissa Ione
FALLING UNDER YOU by Laurelin Paige
EASY FOR KEEPS by Kristen Proby
UNCHAINED by Elisabeth Naughton
HARD TO SERVE by Laura Kaye
DRAGON FEVER by Donna Grant
KAYDEN/SIMON by Alexandra Ivy/Laura Wright
STRUNG UP by Lorelei James
MIDNIGHT UNTAMED by Lara Adrian
TRICKED by Rebecca Zanetti
DIRTY WICKED by Shayla Black
THE ONLY ONE by Lauren Blakely
SWEET SURRENDER by Liliana Hart

Discover 1001 Dark Nights Collection Four

Go to www.1001DarkNights.com for more information.

ROCK CHICK REAWAKENING by Kristen Ashley
ADORING INK by Carrie Ann Ryan
SWEET RIVALRY by K. Bromberg
SHADE'S LADY by Joanna Wylde
RAZR by Larissa Ione
ARRANGED by Lexi Blake
TANGLED by Rebecca Zanetti
HOLD ME by J. Kenner
SOMEHOW, SOME WAY by Jennifer Probst
TOO CLOSE TO CALL by Tessa Bailey
HUNTED by Elisabeth Naughton
EYES ON YOU by Laura Kaye
BLADE by Alexandra Ivy/Laura Wright
DRAGON BURN by Donna Grant
TRIPPED OUT by Lorelei James
STUD FINDER by Lauren Blakely
MIDNIGHT UNLEASHED by Lara Adrian
HALLOW BE THE HAUNT by Heather Graham
DIRTY FILTHY FIX by Laurelin Paige
THE BED MATE by Kendall Ryan
PRINCE ROMAN by CD Reiss
NO RESERVATIONS by Kristen Proby
DAWN OF SURRENDER by Liliana Hart

Also from 1001 Dark Nights

Tempt Me by J. Kenner

About Donna Grant

New York Times and USA Today bestselling author Donna Grant has been praised for her "totally addictive" and "unique and sensual" stories. She's the author of more than eighty novels spanning multiple genres of romance. Her latest acclaimed series, Dark Kings, features dragons, the Fae, and immortal Highlanders who are dark, dangerous, and irresistible.

She lives with her two children, one dog, and four cats in Texas.

For more information about Donna, visit her website at www.DonnaGrant.com or www.MotherofDragonsBooks.com.

Discover More Donna Grant

Dragon Burn
A Dark Kings Novella
By Donna Grant

Marked by passion
A promise made eons ago sends Sebastian to Italy on the hunt to find an enemy. His quarry proves difficult to locate, but there is someone who can point him in the right direction – a woman as frigid as the north. Using every seductive skill he's acquired over his immortal life, his seduction begins. Until he discovers that the passion he stirs within her makes him burn for more...

Gianna Santini has one love in her life – work. A disastrous failed marriage was evidence enough to realize she was better off on her own. That is until a handsome Scot strolled into her life and literally swept her off her feet. She is unprepared for the blazing passion between them or the truth he exposes. But as her world begins to unravel, she realizes the only one she can depend on is the very one destroying everything - a Dragon King.

* * * *

Dragon King
A Dark Kings Novella
By Donna Grant

A Woman On A Mission
Grace Clark has always done things safe. She's never colored outside of the law, but she has a book due and has found the perfect spot to break through her writer's block. Or so she thinks. Right up until Arian suddenly appears and tries to force her away from the mountain. Unaware of the war she just stumbled into, Grace doesn't just discover the perfect place to write, she finds Arian - the most gorgeous, enticing, mysterious man she's ever met.

A King With a Purpose

Arian is a Dragon King who has slept away centuries in his cave. Recently woken, he's about to leave his mountain to join his brethren in a war when he's alerted that someone has crossed onto Dreagan. He's ready to fight...until he sees the woman. She's innocent and mortal - and she sets his blood aflame. He recognizes the danger approaching her just as the dragon within him demands he claim her for his own...

* * * *

Dragon Fever
A Dark Kings Novella
By Donna Grant

A yearning that won't be denied

Rachel Marek is a journalist with a plan. She intends to expose the truth about dragons to the world — and her target is within sight. Nothing matters but getting the truth, especially not the ruggedly handsome, roguishly thrilling Highlander who oozes danger and charm. And when she finds the truth that shatters her faith, she'll have to trust her heart to the very man who can crush it...

A legend in the flesh

Suave, dashing Asher is more than just a man. He's a Dragon King — a being who has roamed this planet since the beginning of time. With everything on the line, Asher must choose to trust an enemy in the form of an all too alluring woman whose tenacity and passion captivate him. Together, Asher and Rachel must fight for their lives — and their love — before an old enemy destroys them both...

Dragon Claimed
A Dark Kings Novella
By Donna Grant
Coming January 15, 2019

Born to rule the skies as a Dragon King with power and magic, Cináed hides his true identity in the mountains of Scotland with the rest of his brethren. But there is no rest for them as they protect their planet and the human occupants from threats. However, a new, more dangerous enemy has targeted the Kings. One that will stop at nothing until the dragons are gone for good. But Cináed finds someone who might know something that could help.

First an orphan and now divorced, Gemma has come to accept that she's meant to spent her life alone. No matter where she lives or what job she takes, she feels…lost. As if she missed the path she was supposed to take. Everything changes when she runs into the most dangerously seductive man she's ever laid eyes. Gemma surrenders to the all-consuming attraction and the wild, impossible love that could destroy them both – and finds her place amid magic and dragons.

On behalf of 1001 Dark Nights,

Liz Berry and M.J. Rose would like to thank ~

Steve Berry
Doug Scofield
Kim Guidroz
Jillian Stein
InkSlinger PR
Dan Slater
Asha Hossain
Chris Graham
Fedora Chen
Kasi Alexander
Jessica Johns
Dylan Stockton
Richard Blake
and Simon Lipskar

94011481R00104

Made in the USA
Middletown, DE
17 October 2018